CHERRY AMES, FLIGHT NURSE

CHERRY AMES NURSE STORIES

CHERRY AMES FLIGHT NURSE

By

HELEN WELLS

New York

Copyright © 1945 by Grosset & Dunlap, Inc.
Copyright © renewed 2007 by Harriet Schulman Forman
Springer Publishing Company, LLC

All rights reserved.

No part of this publication may be reproduced, stored in a retrieval system, or transmitted in any form or by any means, electronic, mechanical, photocopying, recording, or otherwise, without the prior permission of Springer Publishing Company, LLC.

Springer Publishing Company, LLC
11 West 42nd Street, 15th Floor
New York, NY 10036-8002

Acquisitions Editor: Sally J. Barhydt
Production Editor: Matthew Byrd
Cover design by Takeout Graphics, Inc.
Composition: Techbooks

08   09   10/5   4   3   2

Library of Congress Cataloging-in-Publication Data

Wells, Helen, 1910-
  Cherry Ames, flight nurse / by Helen Wells.
    p. cm. — (Cherry Ames nurse stories)
  Summary: With the war still ongoing, Cherry Ames works as a flight nurse, flying into battle zones to pick up wounded soldiers and take them to base hospitals for treatment.
  ISBN 0-8261-0397-9
  [1. Nurses—Fiction.   2. United States. Army Nurse Corps—Fiction.
3. Flight—Fiction.   4. World War, 1939-1945—Fiction.]   I. Title.
PZ7.W4644Ce 2006
[Fic]—dc22

                                                2006022322

Printed in the United States of America by Bang Printing

Contents

	Foreword	vii
I	Practice Flight	1
II	Somewhere in Britain	17
III	Mystery of Mark Grainger	31
IV	"Aunt" Cherry	62
V	First Mission	93
VI	A Medal for Johnny	113
VII	Christmas Party	128
VIII	Under Fire	149
IX	The Mystery Explained	174
X	Mission Home	194

Foreword

Helen Wells, the author of the Cherry Ames stories, said, "I've always thought of nursing, and perhaps you have, too, as just about the most exciting, important, and rewarding, profession there is. Can you think of any other skill that is *always* needed by everybody, everywhere?"

I was and still am a fan of Cherry Ames. Her courageous dedication to her patients; her exciting escapades; her thirst for knowledge; her intelligent application of her nursing skills; and the respect she achieved as a registered nurse (RN) all made it clear to me I was going to follow in her footsteps and become a nurse—nothing else would do. Thousands of other young people were motivated by Cherry Ames to become RNs as well. Cherry Ames motivated young people on into the 1970s, when the series ended. Readers who remember reading these books in the past will enjoy rereading them now—whether or not they chose nursing as a career—and perhaps sharing them with others.

My career has been a rich and satisfying one, during which I have delivered babies, saved lives, and cared for people in hospitals and in their homes. I have worked at the bedside and served as an administrator. I have published journals, written articles, taught students, consulted, and given expert testimony. Never once did I regret my decision to enter nursing.

During the time that I was publishing a nursing journal, I became acquainted with Robert Wells, brother of Helen Wells. In the course of conversation I learned that Ms. Wells had passed on and left the Cherry Ames copyright to Mr. Wells. Because there is a shortage of nurses here in the US today, I thought, "Why not bring Cherry back to motivate a whole new generation of young people? Why not ask Mr. Wells for the copyright to Cherry Ames?" Mr. Wells agreed, and the republished series is dedicated both to Helen Wells, the original author, and to her brother, Robert Wells, who transferred the rights to me. I am proud to ensure the continuation of Cherry Ames into the twenty-first century.

The final dedication is to you, both new and old readers of Cherry Ames: It is my dream that you enjoy Cherry's nursing skills as well as her escapades. I hope that young readers will feel motivated to choose nursing as their life's work. Remember, as Helen Wells herself said: there's no other skill that's "*always* needed by everybody, everywhere."

Harriet Schulman Forman, RN, EdD
Series Editor

CHAPTER I

Practice Flight

LIEUTENANT CHERRY AMES, OF THE ARMY NURSE Corps, training at Randolph Field, Texas, to become a flight nurse, decided to take time out, this hot September morning, for a Coke.

In the PX—the post exchange—Cherry ran into her old friend Ann Evans. Ann, looking pale, was buying chewing gum.

"Why, Annie, you don't chew gum!" Cherry protested.

"No, but my pilot does," Ann replied grimly. "We made a pact. Anyone who gets airsick on training flights has to buy the crew chief six packs of gum. Not only am I flipsy-flopsy in the stomach—I'm going broke!"

Cherry grinned. "You'll outgrow it as I did. Come on over here to the soda fountain and have a cup of tea."

The two girls were perched on stools at the fountain when redheaded Gwen Jones burst in. She waved a special-delivery letter.

"For you, Cherry! I've looked all over for you! Open it quick—it's from Dr. Joe."

Cherry ripped open the letter and scanned the small, neat handwriting—a scientist's hand.

"Hurray! Dr. Joe is coming to our graduation. But something seems to be up. He wants me to—" she read on "—to look for someone and do something when we get overseas—*provided* we are sent to England. He says he can't explain it in a letter." She turned the page over, and examined it again. "That's odd."

"A mystery," Gwen suggested hopefully.

"Rumor sayeth all new flight nurses are slated for England," Ann contributed.

Ann and Gwen, old, dear friends who had been student nurses with Cherry, read the letter, too. Cherry sipped her Coke thoughtfully. Major Joseph Fortune had been Cherry's friend and neighbor from the moment she and her twin brother were born. His motherless daughter, Midge, was practically Cherry's little sister. Cherry was really touched that Dr. Joe was traveling from his Army research laboratory in Washington, D.C., to see her graduated. She knew her family could not come to Texas all the way from Illinois. She was bursting to know what Dr. Joe was referring to in his letter. It was not like him to be mysterious.

"Is Lex, or should I say Captain Upham, coming, too?" Ann asked.

"Your old beau, now Dr. Joe's assistant," Gwen chanted. "My, my, what a change of role!"

Cherry said absently, "Do you know it's almost a year—a year this coming Christmas—since I've seen Lex? It's pretty hard to keep up a friendship by mail."

"Never mind Lex," Ann said. "What's this mystery?"

Cherry shrugged. "We won't know until Dr. Joe gets here."

"How can you wait?" Gwen demanded. "I'm already itching with curiosity and it isn't even *my* who-killed-Cock-Robin."

"I just hope we get to England," Cherry said. "Oh, graduation day, hurry up and get here!"

Between the day the letter arrived and graduation, Cherry had plenty to learn. Here at Randolph Field, Texas, about a ten-minute ride from San Antonio, she attended the Army Air Forces School of Air Evacuation. At this Troop Carrier Command base, teams of AAF doctors, nurses, enlisted medical technicians, and pilots, trained together. They were people of fire and courage. They had to be. Six weeks of intensive work, and then they would be ready to fly, in their winged ambulances, to every American battle front on the globe. They would fly to places where wounded men needed help *fast*—places where only planes could get through. They would pick up the wounded and fly them back to base hospitals. "Flying angels," soldiers called these gallant nurses of the air.

"This is the strangest, most wonderful school I ever saw!" Cherry thought, as she walked across the vast, windy airfield, to meet her pilot, Captain Wade Cooper. Cherry looked up to the sky. It was full of Army planes—her new home was the sky, now.

Parked planes were so thickly clustered that Cherry walked under their wings as often as under blue sky. The air vibrated with the hoarse thunder of plane engines. Dozens of gray planes swooped and roared over her head. Propellers flashed in the sun. Everywhere, aloft and on the earth, were sunburned young men in khaki uniforms, or hard-working young men in green fatigues. Cherry's dark eyes shone. She put one hand on her blouse. She, too, like the young men, would wear silver wings there.

She would also wear the flight nurse's jaunty uniform of slacks, shirt, and side-perched trench cap, in Air Force blue. But now, she ran into the nurses' barracks, and into her room, to slip on her working coveralls.

Cherry's room was small, with fresh-smelling wood walls and a big open window, which gave her the good feeling of living almost outdoors.

"The rooms I've lived in!" she marveled as she changed her clothes.

First and dearest was her own room at home. Home was Hilton, a neighborly Middle West small town,

PRACTICE FLIGHT 5

where Cherry and her twin brother, Charlie, had gone to school together—where they had two of the nicest, liveliest parents anywhere. Yet Cherry had left home, when Dr. Joe had awakened her to the great work of helping people through nursing. Right after high school, Cherry moved into a chintz-and-maple room at Spencer Hospital Nursing School. There, despite a number of scrapes and her stormy romance with Lex, she had proudly earned her R.N.—Registered Nurse. After that, Cherry had lived in Army pup tents, or handsome Army post buildings; in a white marble Castilian castle in Panama, and in rude shacks in the embattled Pacific jungle. For the last six months, awaiting reassignment to volunteer air duty, she had been working in a station hospital in the United States. And now, for a few brief weeks, she occupied this airy little room. Then on to—who knew where? To England, with luck!

"To wherever our wounded soldiers need me," Cherry thought soberly. "To wherever I can keep a man from dying."

Wherever people needed a girl with love in her heart and healing in her hands, that was where Cherry belonged. She wanted to serve, she had trained to serve. Sympathy or vague good intentions—these were not enough for her. Only a nurse, Cherry knew, could bring so much help and comfort and hope to others, who sorely needed her. Only a nurse could experience such broad human adventure, such profound inner reward. She thought for a moment of the other girls who had trained with her at Spencer—Vivian, Bertha, Mai Lee and Josie. "Yes, they're the finest, highest type girls, all of them," Cherry thought. "And they're all Army nurses!" They were now at another camp in the United States, waiting to go overseas again as ground nurses. Cherry crossed her fingers about where her MAE—Medical Air Evacuation—Squadron of twenty-five nurses (divided into four "flights" and a Chief Nurse) might be sent. There were two squadrons, fifty nurses, training together here at Randolph.

Cherry buttoned the final button on her coveralls. She was all ready now for work.

She raced out to the field to find her pilot. He was standing at the plane, talking with the ground crewmen. Cherry liked Captain Wade Cooper. This tall, laughing, sunburned young flier was fun.

"Here comes my nurse!" he hailed her. He left the mechanics, and drew Cherry under the wing. "We're early today. Stick around and talk to me, Lieutenant Ames."

"What'll we talk about?" Cherry teased. She leaned against the huge plane wheel.

"We-ell. What should I say to a nurse?" He grinned candidly. "You know, this is the first time I ever was teamed up with a nurse. We pilots think flight nurses are pretty special."

PRACTICE FLIGHT

"Thank you, Captain. I'm proud to be in the Air Forces. And I'm glad to have drawn you for my superior officer."

"Well, I'm glad too. Now can we drop the formalities?"

They laughed, and Cherry caught a gleam of deviltry in his bright brown eyes.

"When the Chief Nurse introduced us, she said you have quite a famous record. What are you famous for, Captain Cooper?" Cherry asked.

Wade Cooper made a face.

"I'm famous for doing things in a plane that no one in his right mind should do."

"Come on now, tell me.

"Look, Cherry, I'll send you a memo in the morning. Read all about it—Cooper's cutups—only five cents a copy—the twentieth part of a dollah!"

But Cherry teased and coaxed. Captain Cooper had to give in with a grin. When he grinned, Cherry noted, he looked like a happy six-year-old.

It turned out that Wade Cooper, when he was in the bomber command, one day took up a bomber—which normally carries a crew of six or seven—all by himself. Without permission, at reckless risk to his life and to the costly plane, he made a one-man attack on a Japanese base. His instruments and lights were shot out by antiaircraft fire, he was caught in a tropic storm, but he brought the giant plane home, anyhow, singlehanded.

This was an heroic accomplishment, but against orders. He had already been warned, time and again, about taking crazy chances—for fun.

"I guess I was something of a smart aleck. Jeepers, what a time I had for myself! When you fly one of those high-powered bombers, why, you're just sitting there with a thousand horses in your lap and a feather in your tail!"

"Why did they put you, of all people, in an ambulance plane? That's one place where you'll have to fly safe and sane."

"That was the general idea. They transferred me to the aerial ambulances to teach me a lesson—to *make* me fly safely." He groaned.

"You're not very enthusiastic about being here."

"Might as well hitch a race horse to a grocery wagon."

"Maybe I can make you see that flying the patients is mighty exciting work too."

"Well, having you aboard my plane, Lieutenant Cherry, is going to make up for a lot!"

Now Cherry asked a favor which she had had on her mind for some days—ever since she heard a certain pleasant piece of news. She explained to her pilot that a very fine medical technician she knew was training at Randolph Field. His name was Bunce Smith. He was not yet assigned to a team, and Cherry wondered if Captain Cooper would ask for the young technician.

"Sure thing. I'll go right over and request to have him placed in my crew. You wait here."

In ten minutes, the flier returned with Bunce. Bunce was still a tall, lanky, gangling youngster, and he was grinning from ear to ear.

"Miss Cherry! Jehosophat, I'm glad to see you!"

"Bunce, this is wonderful!"

He shook her hand so long and hard he nearly pumped off her arm. Cherry looked delightedly at her former corpsman. Bunce had grown up some, though not much. His clothes no longer hung perilously on him; his uniform fit neatly and there were now sergeant's stripes on his sleeve. However, his hands and feet were still outsize and still in his way, and his light brown hair still had a cowlick that would not lie down. His blue eyes beamed at Cherry.

"Look, I'm still wearing that Indian ring you gave me."

"Wearing sergeant's stripes, too, I see. Want to be on my team?"

"Do I? Wow! When do we start?"

Captain Cooper grinned at both of them. "Seems you know each other from way back when."

Bunce offered solemnly, "Miss Cherry reformed me once, sir. It was a pleasure."

The flier shoved his hands in his pockets. "Ma'am, I see where you're going to reform me, if I'm not careful."

They all laughed. Cherry asked her corpsman:

"What's been happening to you, anyway? And what's this ribbon on your shirt? Are you a hero, Bunce?"

"Shucks, no, Miss Cherry. When I was a litter-bearer in the field, I just went out and got some beat-up fellows and they gave me this fruit salad."

"You mean you rescued the wounded under fire."

"Well—sort of—yes. Three or four times."

Cherry turned to Captain Cooper, who had whistled softly. "Did you hear that modest account, Captain?"

"Wait till I tell my crew about this pill roller."

Two young AAF men joined them. They all exchanged cordial hellos, and Cherry introduced her medical technician. The copilot, Wade's assistant, was Lieutenant William Mason, a sunburned young man with the sharp eyes of a flier. Lieutenant Richard Greenberg, radioman and navigator, was a quiet, gray-eyed boy who looked efficient. His job was to transmit messages and to keep the plane on the right course.

Wade, Bill, Dick, Bunce made up Cherry's flight team. That ended the informality. Once at work, they were Captain, Lieutenant, and Sergeant.

The plane thrilled Cherry. The muddy-colored giant had four motors and a wingspread of nearly a block on each side. This Douglas C-47, called the Skytrain and "work horse of the air," was a transport cargo plane. In peace, it had carried passengers or freight; in war, the Army had converted it to carry jeeps and tanks and troops—or patients. When Cherry's team flew to battle

PRACTICE FLIGHT 11

areas to pick up the wounded, they would never fly an empty plane but would haul troops or vital cargo. With such military cargo, they would have no right to the protection of a Red Cross painted on their aircraft. Instead, the white star of American combat forces was painted on its broad dark side.

"We'll be a fair target for the enemy," Cherry realized.

Up in the plane's side, in the middle, were huge, double bay doors. Pushed up to them was a portable ramp. There was also a tractor-elevator which lifted two stretchers at a time up to the doors.

Inside, up forward in the nose, and closed off by a door, was the pilot's cockpit and just off this, the radio compartment. In the rear compartment, through a door leading into the tail, was a space for medical supplies, and a tiny galley. They would always take along fruit juice, water and coffee in their sky kitchen.

The long body of the plane comprised the cabin. It had arching, ribbed, steel walls and a corrugated floor. In the low roof were flat ceiling lights. It was like being inside a tunnel or in a narrow steel freight car. Yet Cherry learned fascinatedly that this long cabin could be made into a temporary hospital ward.

The walls were partitioned off, on either side, into three sections. In each section, stowed away in canvas containers on the walls, were four webbing-strap litter supports, at four different heights. These strong straps were pulled down, and a litter or stretcher was placed across them, parallel to the plane wall. The four litters went one above the other, bunk or Pullman fashion, from the floor to the ceiling. This left an aisle down the middle of the plane. There were additional straps to keep the patients from falling out of their stretchers.

In case Cherry flew ambulatory patients, that is, patients who could walk and sit up, she would break down a section of litters and put up four bucket seats instead. These, too, pulled down from the wall. She would always reserve one seat for herself and one for the medical technician, because on take-offs or landings, everyone must sit down and strap in. Cherry was warned never to take off her safety belt until the plane had leveled off.

Cherry's chief pride was her nurse's medicine chest in the rear compartment. This big seventy-two pound metal suitcase contained enough supplies for a small hospital. In addition to all the usual medicines for relief of pain, stimulants, sedatives, bandages, splints, there was also blood plasma, whole-blood units and equipment for intravenous medication.

Cherry also carried an eighteen pound medical kit. She could zip it open and hang it on the cargo door of the plane, so that everything was within easy reach.

"Besides the standard supplies," Cherry told Bunce, "I'll decide what special supplies we'll need for particular patients on each trip. After I have a look at the wounded men we're going to fly, I'll ask you to get those supplies for me from the doctor. We'll do that while we're loading the patients aboard."

Cherry also had a talk with Wade Cooper. Some of the wounded would be apprehensive about flying. It would reassure them if the pilot made a little speech before the take-off.

Wade fretted. "I'm a pilot—not a nursemaid! Besides, what'll I say?"

"Oh, just say—" Cherry assumed the deepest, gruffest voice she could "—'Men, I'm your pilot. Don't worry, because I've had plenty of flying experience. For instance, I've flown in—uh—in—' "

"In China and over the Hump," Wade supplied casually.

"Oh! Did you really? Well, then, *I'll* say, 'Fellows, besides being experienced, Captain Cooper is a particularly careful flier. Isn't that so, Captain Cooper?'" Cherry tried hard to keep a straight face.

Wade gave her an exasperated look out of the corner of his eye. "Then I'll say, 'I'll try to be particularly careful.' " He grunted.

"Cautious. No recklessness. Responsible. Safe and sane," Cherry persisted gleefully. "That's Captain Cooper all over. Isn't it, Captain?"

"A fine thing! A fine thing they're doing to me! Me—a bomber pilot! Telling me to be careful, be cautious, everything but stop for a cow to cross the road!"

With her crew and a reluctant pilot, Cherry practiced loading and unloading perfectly healthy GI's. She had classroom lectures, too.

A Flight Surgeon, their commanding officer at Randolph, was one of the nurses' several instructors. Major La Rosa talked quietly but forcefully.

"Air evacuation is a modern miracle—a fusion of medicine and aviation. Now, you Army nurses already know how to care for your patients on the ground. But take a sick or wounded person up into thin air, and his condition changes. A man with a chest or abdominal wound could rapidly get worse, even die, above eight thousand feet. You may have to fly very high, to avoid bad weather or the enemy. So you must have special knowledge to treat sick and wounded at various altitudes."

Cherry listened, fascinated, as a new world—a world of high, empty thin air—was born in her imagination. A world of wind and empty space, one or two or three miles above the earth, so high up there was nothing at all, nothing but the sun or the moon. In that nothingness, a plane would be streaking along, with its precious cargo of wounded, suffering soldiers, and a nurse to keep watch over them.

"You, the flight nurse, will be in complete medical charge on the trip," Major La Rosa said. "From the time you pick up the wounded in the combat zone, until you unload them at the base hospital, you alone are responsible for the lives of eighteen wounded soldiers. Of course, you will have your medical or flight technician to assist you. With the pilot and his crew of two to fly the plane, you'll all work together as a team. The Flight Surgeon will help you, but only when the plane is on the ground."

So Cherry had to learn to manage everything by herself, once the flying ambulance was in the air.

Cherry already knew how to arrest hemorrhage, dress wounds, adjust splints, set fractures temporarily, administer blood plasma and give shock treatment. Now she learned how to do all these things, never easy, under the difficult and special conditions of flight. She learned that patients with head injuries must be flown at as low an altitude as possible—that chest injuries require oxygen at any altitude—that certain medicines must be adjusted to certain altitudes—and she learned when to substitute the rules with her own good sense. Flying would cause one patient to need a stimulant, but another patient a sedative. What impressed Cherry was that she must treat each case as a special problem and keep constant watch over each one of them!

During these six weeks, Cherry and her classmates were up at six, at work by seven, and working until six or seven at night—Sundays too. Cherry felt as if she were performing in a three-ring circus, but she thrived on it. Gwen declared good-naturedly that this school was "a concentration camp on our side."

16   *CHERRY AMES, FLIGHT NURSE*

Cherry was more surprised than frightened when she was marched to the top of a thirty-foot tower, shown how to jump, fall, and to "hit the silk"—use a parachute.

She was goggle-eyed when the nurses, in full uniform with pistols and medical kits, were ordered to clamber out of a floating "forced-down" plane in the post's vast swimming pool, and to keep themselves and their husky "patients" afloat.

She found herself swimming through burning gasoline and oil, finally to emerge scared but unharmed.

She struggled through a hair-raising simulated plane accident which was casually listed as "crash procedure."

"Home was never like this," said Cherry.

Then Cherry took eleven examinations.

Finally, she put on her good flying suit, which was slacks and blouse of blue-gray gabardine, and her garrison cap, carefully packed her parachute, and went traveling in a C-47 across the United States. She served as an aide to the flight nurse in charge, on an actual air evacuation mission. Two days later, Cherry got off the plane at Randolph Field. She was dirty and dead-tired but sure now that she knew her job.

"Now," thought Cherry. "Now!" At last the gruelling six weeks training was over—and now she was going to receive her wings and to see Dr. Joe.

CHAPTER II

Somewhere in Britain

ONLY TWENTY-FOUR HOURS LAY BETWEEN CHERRY'S graduation and her departure for overseas. Rumors flew among the fifty flight nurses in the two new squadrons. "We're going to England." "No, we're slated for Alaska." "At least we're not going to the Pacific theater, we've already served there." "They've issued us flying suits for a moderate climate, so it's England for sure!"

As Cherry packed in her airy little barracks room, and wrote her last letters home, she wondered what her destination would be. Somehow she felt that her squadron would be stationed in Britain. The breathtakingly hard job that lay ahead troubled her. She had trained hard and well, had passed her examinations, but when it came to the real thing, the ultimate ordeal—

"I'll just have to call upon every resource I have, body, mind, and soul," Cherry thought. "I won't think of myself; I won't listen to these doubts. I'll think of the boys I'm there to help. That, if anything, will carry me through."

The evening before graduation day, Cherry took a bus into San Antonio, to the railroad station. When Dr. Fortune stepped off the train, he looked the same as ever. Cherry ran happily to the vague-minded little man, with the lock of gray hair falling boyishly over one eye.

"Dr. Joe! Oh, I'm so glad to see someone from home!"

"Bless your heart, Cherry. I'm glad to see you, too," and he kissed her on the forehead.

Cherry laughed happily. Then the realization that Lex had not come along flashed through her mind. It gave her a little pang.

"You look tired, Dr. Joe, too tired," Cherry said concernedly.

"I'm fine—fine." But his seamed face and thoughtful eyes betrayed signs of fatigue and worry. He made an effort to brighten up. "Midge instructed me to send you her 'most profound regards.' Lex did the same, and I have a box of vitamins for you. I also brought you an identification bracelet as a graduation gift, but you may not have it until tomorrow."

Having recollected all he was supposed to say, Dr. Joe fell silent. He stood on the station platform rather helplessly, holding his hat.

Cherry smiled. "Thank you, sir, but come along now! We'll take a bus back to post, then I'll get you installed in the guest house, and feed you some dinner."

"I want to talk with you, Cherry," he said seriously.

That evening, in a quiet corner of the Officers' Club, they talked in low tones.

"I have a friend in England who is in trouble," Dr. Joe began, in his deep, slow voice. "I can't make out from the censored letters exactly what the trouble is." He explained that some years ago, through his university contacts, he had met and come to be friends with an English family. The son-in-law, Mark Grainger, was an engineer and had come to the United States to attend graduate engineering school. With Mark Grainger had come his lovely young wife, Lucia, and Lucia's mother, Mark's mother-in-law, widowed Mrs. Eldredge.

"They were fine people. I liked them, particularly the spirited old lady, though she can be difficult to deal with. It's she who has been writing to me—about Mark."

"What has Mark done?"

"Let me tell you the whole story first."

The English family had returned to Britain when it looked as if their country might be attacked. Mark joined the British Army and was stationed in England. The next thing Dr. Joe heard was that Mark and Lucia had had a baby girl. Then the Germans bombed London. Dr. Joe wrote and wrote, wondering if his friends were still alive. At last came a heartbroken letter from Mrs. Eldredge. Her daughter Lucia had died, when her house was struck by a bomb and she had been buried in the cave-in. The baby girl, then a year or two old, was rescued from the burning ruins.

"What's the baby's name?" Cherry asked breathlessly.

"I don't recall. At any rate, she's not a baby now. She must be about six—six or seven."

Cherry found herself thinking not of the adults but of the little girl, who had been so miraculously saved. That child could not remember her mother, had never known anything but the terror and privation of war. Poor little tyke!

"Do you know where your friends are now, Dr. Joe?"

"The grandmother and the little girl are living in a country village a couple of hours' ride north of London. You know, they evacuated the children from the cities, to safer country places. Fortunately Mrs. Eldredge and the youngster were not separated—as so many families were."

"And Mark Grainger?"

Dr. Joe pushed back his lock of gray hair. "That's the curious thing. That's what Mrs. Eldredge is suspicious about."

"Suspicious—of her own son-in-law? Of that child's father?"

Dr. Joe shrugged. "I find it hard to believe anything wrong of Mark Grainger. Besides, Mrs. Eldredge doesn't dare write about all this in any detail. All I know is that he is no longer in the British Army, and that Mrs. Eldredge is very much disturbed about something."

"It is odd," Cherry agreed. But her thoughts strayed back to the little girl.

"Now this is what I want you to do, Cherry, if you will. There is an American Army air base north of London, very near the village where Mrs. Eldredge and the little Grainger girl live. It's likely that you may be stationed there, from what I know. If you are, and if you have the chance, find out what you can. Do what you can to help those people. But—" Dr. Joe hesitated, then looked at her quizzically, "be discreet."

"Discreet? Oh, yes, Dr. Joe, I'll be the soul of discretion," Cherry promised. "But why...?"

"Cherry, child," Dr. Joe got to his feet, "that is all I know. Just promise me you'll help if you can."

Cherry tossed back her black curls and rose too. "As if I'd ever say 'No' to you! Of course I promise, Dr. Joe."

"Now off to sleep! Tomorrow is going to be your big day."

Graduation was hurried but inspiring. The new flight nurses filed into the lovely little chapel, knowing this was their great and perilous beginning. The chaplain's prayer for their safekeeping sank deep into their hearts. Cherry heard the school's Commandant praise their courage. He reminded them that they were not only nurses, but also soldiers with wings.

Then, in a simple ceremony, each bright-eyed nurse stood at attention while the Colonel presented diplomas and pinned miniature Flight Surgeon's wings—of silver, with the superimposed N—on each girl's slate-blue jacket. Cherry cherished her silver wings as the proudest possession of her entire life. She saw that Ann and Gwen, even the experienced ex-stewardess, Agnes Gray, felt the same solemn happiness. Together, they all renewed their nurse's pledge, and sang the stirring song of the flight nurses.

The Commandant said, "I am sorry there is no time for celebrations. You will be assigned at once."

Immediately upon leaving the chapel, the two new squadrons were staged. Cherry did not even have time to say good-bye to Dr. Joe, nor to telephone her mother long-distance, nor to hunt up Wade or Bunce. Cherry had expected this. She calmly accepted her sealed orders and as calmly boarded a northbound train, that night.

The nurses were whisked through New York next day to a pier, and promptly sent up the gangplank of a troop transport. Once a luxury liner, this huge steamer was crowded, deck upon deck, from stem to stern, with young men in Army uniform. Some of the fellows hanging over the deck rail whistled at the nurses. The nurses smiled at them and waved friendly hellos.

The nurses waited in the ship's lounge, amid bright electric lights and piles of luggage, for cabin assignments. An officer came up and started reading off their names.

"Ames, Evans, Gray, Hortas, Jones, Wiegand—you're Flight Three—Cabin 27 on B deck."

Cherry and Ann and Gwen exchanged glances. These other three were to be not only their bunkmates for the voyage, but also their permanent mates in their flight group of six nurses! Cherry was pleased that the one-time stewardess, Agnes Gray, was in her flight. Lieutenant Gray was pleasant, and she was the calm veteran of seventeen hundred hours flying time. Gwen went to find the other two. Elsie Wiegand was tall and fair and looked like a good scout. Margaret Hortas, a small, dark girl, seemed to be perishing of shyness. They had seen one another at Randolph Field, but there had been no time there for real acquaintance.

Cherry tried to break the ice by saying, "Elsie... Agnes... Margaret... Let's see. That would make you Aggie and Maggie."

Everyone laughed. Lieutenant Wiegand whispered, "Look over there! Inside that soldier-musician's French horn. He's smuggling a dog aboard inside the horn!"

They made their way through the ship's narrow corridors and found Cabin 27—a room originally intended for three. Now there were three regular beds, one of them a second-story bunk, and three Army cots in the room. Cherry was relieved to see that not one nurse in her flight made a selfish dash for a bed instead of a cot. They good-humoredly flipped coins to see who would sleep where. Cherry drew a cot, and was perfectly satisfied.

All six nurses of Flight Three sat down on their respective beds (except Margaret, who was small and refused offers to be hoisted to her second-story bunk) and proceeded to play Truth. Cherry started it off.

"I'm from a small town in Illinois, went to Spencer Nursing School, and nursed in the Army Nurse Corps in Panama and in the Pacific."

"Ditto for me," said Ann Evans. "I—I have a fiancé in the Army."

"Ditto for me," said Gwen, nodding her red head, "except no fiancé and I come from a Pennsylvania mining town where my father is the town doctor. I guess that's not so ditto after all!"

Lieutenant Wiegand's light eyes danced. "I'm from Minnesota, up north in the wheat country. I trained in St. Paul, and I nearly melted away in the heat when the Army sent me to nurse in Brazil."

"Brazil!" they all exclaimed.

"The Pacific!" the tall fair-haired girl exclaimed right back at them. "Now Aggie and Maggie."

The small, dark nurse needed urging. "I'm from California, the San Joachim valley. I trained in the Cadet Nurse Corps—on a scholarship, you know—and I've nursed only in Army camps in the United States." Lieutenant Hortas said hesitantly, "I've never been overseas." She hesitated again, and a gnomish grin spread over her face. "I'm really lots more capable than I look."

"You're probably a pint-sized dynamo," Lieutenant Agnes Gray said generously. She was a little older than the rest, very poised, very pretty and trim, with neat brown hair and brown eyes. "Aggie" was a New Englander. She had flown on one of the civil transcontinental airlines for several years, before she became an Army nurse, and had been through three major crashes without a scratch. The other girls, though, like Cherry, were new to flying.

They joked about Aggie's broad A, and Ann's and Cherry's twangy Midwest accent, their assorted names, and whether any of them snored. Agnes asked hopefully if anyone played bridge. Ann offered to lend any and all comers her tiny iron and board. Cherry passed around seasick tablets. They all debated whether a steward would bring a ladder for the upper bunk or whether they would have to hoist Maggie up and down. By the time the bell rang—for what they hoped was noonday dinner—and they went above, the nurses of Flight Three were friends.

In the lounge, Cherry saw their Chief Nurse, Captain Betty Ryan. She was a smiling, curly-haired young woman in flight nurse uniform, a flier herself, small and very feminine—and very businesslike.

"Hello, Flight Three!" she greeted them. "Do you all know each other by now? All settled in your cabin?" She looked excited. "I've just found three old friends—nurses. There are two ground units crossing with us."

Cherry pricked up her ears. "Maybe we'll find someone we know, too." For her old classmates, Vivian and Bertha and Mai Lee and Marie Swift, had written that they, too, were going to the European theater, with a mobile evacuation unit.

"We certainly could find romance," observed Lieutenant Agnes Gray. "Did you *ever* see so many officers?"

There were at least three hundred Army, Navy and Medical officers, all looking amiable. Ann asked if the pilots and medical technicians were crossing on this transport with them.

"Our technicians are aboard," Captain Betty said. "But they're below and probably can't come up to visit us. Our pilots and crews are flying the C-47's across—loaded to the seams with medical supplies."

Cherry crossed her fingers, and hoped Wade and his two lieutenants made the transocean flight without mishap. She thought of Bunce down in the hold with the infantrymen.

A crew member came up and said that the Medical Commanding Officer wanted to see the nurses in the foyer. The nurses turned the corner into the foyer and found a tall, gaunt Lieutenant-Colonel awaiting them.

"Nurses," he said, "we are in constant danger of torpedoes from submarines. Once we are at sea, never leave your stateroom without your canteen full of water. That water might have to last you some time in a lifeboat. You are to wear slacks and sweaters during the trip, and sleep in all your clothes at night. That's an order! We will blackout at night, except for very dim lights in the lounge. Life belts will be issued to you; keep them with you every moment. We will have lifeboat drills, so that in case we have to abandon ship it can be done quickly and efficiently. Be vigilant. I hope you enjoy the trip."

As they were all dismissed, Gwen whispered to her flight, "Then the wolf chewed up all the little children. Good night, kiddies, sweet dreams!"

"Oh, we'll have fun, anyway," Cherry said cheerfully. "We always do!"

Late that night, long after the nurses of Flight Three had snuggled into their bunks, the ship put out to sea. Cherry woke suddenly when she felt the enormous darkened liner vibrating, heard the hooting of tugboat whistles, smelled a saltier breeze. Then past their black porthole, the lights of New York slipped away. They shoved out into complete darkness. Cherry cried a little, secretly, into her pillow. She thought she heard sniffles from the other beds, too.

They had a rough crossing, on the turbulent gray October seas. Their ship took a northern route: that meant England. The emptiness stunned Cherry. Everywhere she looked, there was only sky and water, and the empty rim of the horizon.

To Cherry, those five gray, dangerous, storm-tossed days and nights had the quality of a dream, swift and unreal. She went up to mess or attended drill with her companions, danced and chatted with the officers, and helped poor Ann and Maggie through violent seasickness. But her thoughts leaped ahead to her destination. That was more real to her than even a bitter storm on deck, with waves and rain and wind lashing her. Only two incidents occurred during the voyage.

Early one morning, at five-thirty, a violent lurch of the ship and a sharp blast of the ship's whistle tore them out of their beds. They hurried sleepily up the steep companionways to their lifeboat station for another one of those drills. But this was no mere drill. For an hour later, at dawn, the officers took the nurses on deck and showed them sinister debris floating in the ship's wake. A German submarine had shot a torpedo under water at their bow. The ship's personnel had detected it by instrument, and the captain had instantly swerved the huge liner out of its path. They had been saved by seconds and inches. The floating bits were what were left of the submarine.

The other incident occurred when they were getting up into the rough Irish Sea and the steamer was plowing through it like a roller coaster. An Army plane flew over their smokestacks and kept circling. Cherry rushed out on deck with the handful who still had their sea legs. "Mail!" someone shouted as the large canvas bag hit the deck.

There was a letter for Cherry from Dr. Joe. "The child's name is Muriel Grainger. She and Mrs. Hugh (Frances) Eldredge live at forty-one Kelcey Road," and he gave the name of the English village. He enclosed a rather cloudy snapshot of a little girl with enormous, solemn eyes, standing at a gate.

"Hello, Muriel," Cherry said silently to the mite in the snapshot. "I'm going to find you and help you if I can!"

Then she reread with quickened interest the lively booklet which the War Department issued to all soldiers going to Great Britain, describing the people they were going to meet.

One day more, with skies and seas clearing, and then on the empty horizon line appeared a blot of land. Scotland! Next day gulls flew past and they saw other ships.

The nurses were lined up, laden with helmets, mess kits, and suitcases, for final instructions. The same tall Lieutenant-Colonel addressed them.

"We are about to enter a foreign country. No matter how strange things may. seem to you, do not criticize. We Americans, barging into these people's homeland, seem strange to them. They will judge our country by us. Each one of us must be an ambassador of good will. Try to be understanding, always be kind and pleasant, above all be courteous." He added, "Anyone who is not will be punished. Forward, march!"

Down the long gangplank, along a dock, and into a waiting train, marched Cherry and her fellow nurses.

They had never seen a train of this type, with glassed in compartments. Flight Three had its own compartment, crammed full of young women and luggage. Scottish women came through and, out of their limited food supplies, gave the American nurses pancakes and tea. Outside on the platform someone was playing a bagpipe. The train started to move. Cherry stared out the window at cottages and gardens, a bombed-out street in ashes, fields of red flowers. Everyone on the way waved and held his fingers in a V for victory. At sundown the trainmaster poked his head in their compartment and said, "No lights." They were very near the enemy now; their train might be bombed. It grew dark and foggy, then suddenly damp and cold. They finished the pancakes hungrily. The six nurses huddled together for warmth, all the long night.

Next morning Cherry awoke to see the sun slowly rising and heavy dew glistening on a green field. The temperature was warmer, even inside the compartment. The first thatched roofs of a village began slipping by their windows.

Cherry shook the others. "Ann and Gwen! Elsie! Wake up, all of you! We're in England."

CHAPTER III

~~~~~~

Mystery of Mark Grainger

CHERRY BLINKED AND LOOKED AGAIN. YES, FLIGHT Three's grim Army barracks actually was bright purple. The soldiers, at this American Troop Carrier Command of the —th Air Force in Britain, had painted Nurses' Quarters this violent hue as greeting and as, presumably, a feminine touch.

The six girls crowded into their room in the barracks. Although there was a pleasant big sitting room next door, this room was tiny. There were six iron beds jammed together, one dresser, a few hooks nailed on the purple walls. The girl could just about squeeze in themselves and their suitcases.

"I'm going to get us a goldfish bowl and six goldfish," Gwen declared.

Ann shivered. "There's no heat in here."

Elsie reminded her, "There's no heat anywhere in wartime Britain. Cheerio!" And she matter-of-factly donned an extra sweater and a wool muffler.

"Purple!" Cherry muttered. "Of all colors, purple!"

Suddenly it struck them funny. They had a good laugh, then powdered their noses and went to meet their new Commanding Officer.

On the way, they took a good look at the base. It was a bomber base, from which bomber planes and their fighter escorts flew out across the Channel, to attack the enemy. The huge airdrome, a working station in this otherwise green and decorative countryside, swarmed with men of the Army Air Forces. Planes were everywhere, squadrons on the ground, in the air, rolling along the wide air strips. Enormous, camouflaged hangars, repair shops and operational buildings hulked against the peaceful trees and hedges. The landing section was cleared, though it was disguised by false hedge lines and dummy farmhouses. All the other buildings were spread through an old grove of giant shade trees. Steel Nissen huts, low concrete AAF barracks, wooden mess halls, half-submerged air raid shelters, stretched out for a couple of miles under the serene old elms and chestnut trees. Farther away, surrounded by smaller hospital buildings, stood a large brick hospital, its American flag and Red Cross flag fluttering in the balmy breeze.

MYSTERY OF MARK GRAINGER 33

At the hospital, Colonel Lenquist, surgeon, and commander of this Troop Carrier Command Air Evacuation station, greeted the two new squadrons of flight nurses. He explained to them how their first assignments—practice missions—would work out.

"The wounded and sick who may recover within a month stay at a mobile hospital in the combat area. If they need two months for recovery they are transported from the fighting area in Europe to a base hospital, such as ours. If longer care is needed, they are sent back to America. The most urgent cases are chosen to fly back to the States.

"You see how crowded our hospital is. We try to move them out fast to make room for the new casualties coming in. You will fly these patients from here to the transfer hospital in Prestwick, Scotland. Then stay with your plane and return here to home base. Major Thorne will be your Flight Surgeon. I am assigning you to the same teams with which you trained."

Cherry was glad to hear that she would be working with Captain Wade Cooper and Bunce Smith again. She located Bunce and talked to him on the telephone. After some involved efforts, she and Wade finally met in the Red Cross canteen that afternoon.

Out of a knot of chatting pilots, Wade Cooper came over to her, with long, fast, easy strides. His brown eyes, his whole brown face, were alight.

"My long-lost Nurse!" He thumped her affectionately on the shoulder. "How've you been?"

"Captain, I beg to report that I'm fine. How are you? Have a good flight over?"

"Perfect. Everything went off as slick as a whistle." He screwed up his eyes with enthusiasm and jerked up his hands in a perfect circle to show her. "Perfect. One hundred and fifty per cent. Now that you're here, things couldn't be nicer."

Cherry laughed. "You do say the nicest things, but I don't believe you."

"What do you mean! I'm not kidding! I'm darned glad to see you! Like this—" Wade swept his arm around her, kissed her soundly and—while she was still gasping—pulled her toward the door. "C'mon, I'll show you around."

Cherry's cheeks were crimson and her dark curls fell in her eyes.

"Just a minute, Captain," Cherry blurted and righted her trench cap. "The love department doesn't come under your command."

Wade grinned. "We'll see about that!"

Cherry had to smile, even as she reproached him. "Everyone in this canteen is looking at us."

"Let 'em look. They probably envy me. C'mon." He held the door open for her and they went outdoors, and walked along under the leafy roof of magnificent trees.

MYSTERY OF MARK GRAINGER 35

"Stays green and warm a long time here in England," Wade observed. "We'll have fog here, no sun for days on end, but no bitter cold like at home."

"Just the same, you might be wearing a jacket—not just that shirt," Cherry said.

"You too!" Wade pulled his officer's cap down on his forehead in exasperation. "Doggone this safety stuff! Every time we pilots move to a new field, Cherry, we get examined all over again, before they'll let us take up a plane. Heart. Eyes. Balance. Reflexes. It makes me nervous. Sometimes I think I go up and fly in spite of the doctors."

"You pilots are pretty precious," Cherry said lightly. She understood, however, that a flier works under a terrific strain, and that even one small additional strain, like these necessary examinations, was hard on Wade. She resolved to try never to do or say anything which would upset her flier. There was one thing, though, she had to know.

"Wade, did you ever crack up in a plane?" Cherry asked.

"Yes, once. But I went right up again so I didn't have a chance to lose my nerve. Don't look at me as if I were a hero! It's all in the day's work."

Wade showed her through the pilots' club with its bar, game room and open veranda. Cherry guessed that pilots were given more luxuries than any of the other Army forces. When Wade smuggled her down a hallway, for a glimpse into the ready room, she understood the reason. Here sat rows of fliers, elaborately at ease, as they were briefed. They were going out in a few minutes on a bombing mission. Some of them would never come back.

Cherry and Wade went out on the field to watch the bomber squadron take off. The sweating ground crewmen, with anxious faces, were putting the last loving touches on the big brown B-17's, checking up on the bomb load in the plane's belly. The fliers climbed in, joking. Cherry saw how young they all were—some were still in their teens.

The propellers whipped up a big wind. Cherry's khaki skirt lashed, and she and Wade had to shout over the noise. The white signal flag dropped. One by one, the planes taxied, rose, then went thundering overhead in perfect formation. They diminished beyond the trees and blurred into the light in the sky.

"Good luck," Wade said under his breath. "Wish I were going with you."

"Wade—Wade—" Cherry did not know how to express the terrible excitement she felt. "I'd like to stand right here and make sure they—all come back. As if waiting for them—hoping for them—would bring them home."

"That," the pilot smiled a little, "is known as sweating them in. You're going to do a lot of that, living at a bomber base."

"I'll never hear those planes go out and be able to rest until—"

"Here, here, none of that," he said gaily and took her arm. "You don't burst out crying when you see a wounded boy, do you? It'd be the worst thing you could do to him. No, you just do your job for him. Now, my little landlubber, you have a very urgent date with a Coke—or an English version thereof."

The date with a Coke turned into a party. They ran into Agnes and Ann and some of the other nurses with their pilots. A bevy of fighter pilots gravitated to the new nurses. Wade, pretending reluctance, introduced them to Cherry. She was touched by their genuine admiration and respect for flight nurses. One of them said:

"You flight nurses are our real pin-up girls. When we salute you, we aren't just following Army custom. We mean those salutes."

A quieter pilot added, "Let me tell you, Lieutenant Ames, and it's no exaggeration to say this, you flight nurses mean the difference between life and death to many a soldier. I was in North Africa when the hospital planes came in. I know."

Praise, such as this and from such men, filled Cherry—and for that matter, all the nurses—with a warm, strong desire to perform heroic exploits. Upon rising the next morning, they looked forward eagerly to six o'clock which might bring them their first flight assignment. But unfortunately, six A.M. brought only calisthenics and drill, breakfast, house cleaning, and then an all-morning lecture by their Flight Surgeon, Major Thorne. He was a plump, ruddy little man with a twinkle in his eye. In closing the lecture he said:

"I know you ladies are eager for your first flight order. I wish I didn't have to disappoint you. Until your individual flight orders come through, you will do hospital duty. In fact, whenever you have time between flights, we'll need you in the hospital."

The nurses groaned. So they weren't going to fly at once! They had, apparently, crossed an ocean merely to help out on a ward! Major Thorne let them groan and then said:

"As a consolation prize, ladies, you are invited to take the afternoon off. There are several beautiful little English villages within cycling or hitchhiking distance of here. Go and explore and have yourselves a tea party!"

That was very pleasant consolation. Flight Three dressed themselves in their formal khaki jackets and skirts, and went off to pay a call on the nearest English village. A mail corporal gave them a lift in his jeep.

They rode along a narrow, gently winding road, past massive rugged old trees and lovely meadows laced with crystal streams. "It's like fairyland," Maggie murmured.

Cherry breathed in deeply of the fresh sweet air, but she was thinking of something else. She wondered if, by any chance, the village they were on their way to visit would turn out to be the village where Mrs. Eldredge lived. Cherry had not yet learned the names and locations of the surrounding villages. She was disinclined to ask the jeep driver, nor did she want to discuss it with the other girls. The trouble Mrs. Eldredge was facing might be of a confidential nature. Dr. Joe had warned her to be "discreet." Cherry decided, "I won't try to do more this afternoon than get my bearings in a strange place."

So she leaned back between Ann and Gwen, and drank in the sight of sun and leaves and dappled shadows, and enjoyed herself.

Their first glimpse of the little town was a curtain of protective barrage balloons, low in the sky, attached to cables. These helped fend off enemy planes. They saw three houses with roofs missing. In another house they looked in through a broken wall and saw a woman, wearing her coat, cooking at a stove. But at the village square, where the jeep driver called "Last stop!", they found themselves in a kind of storybook village.

"It must be a movie set," Gwen insisted, as they all stood and stared. "It can't be real."

Elsie planted her feet firmly on the ground, industriously opened her guidebook, and read aloud, "Forty-five million people live on this small crowded island. The need for privacy has made them reserved. The Magna Charta was the first democratic bill of rights—"

"Elsie! We can do that later!"

Elsie thumbed through the book. "I had the wrong page. No place in England," she read brightly, "is more than a hundred miles from the sea. There is a great variety of scenery. The—"

"Well, *look* at the scenery!"

"—Tower of London is a thousand years old, and—"

"It's positively dreamy," Agnes Gray crooned to herself. "Oh, do you suppose we'll be permitted to take pictures?"

Cherry and Ann were murmuring, "It's lovely, lovely!"

Nestled in a green valley, this village, with its low ancient buildings, was like a jewel cupped in a setting. A mellow patina of age had softened and deepened all the colors. The rosy bricks of the many-chimneyed houses were overgrown with rustling ivy, shaded by massive trees. Plaster cottages with steep, sloping, thatched roofs and dormer windows sat amidst gardens. The pub—public house—and the Fish and Chips shop displayed curious many-paned windows, and worn stone doorsteps that must have known the tread of the people of Elizabethan times. The silvery-gray fieldstone church, of exquisite and simple design, stood in the heart of the village, facing the single winding tree-lined street, High Street. Along the lanes were gardens and hedges ripe with centuries of cultivation. Over everything hung a serenity and dignity, even in wartime, which was very impressive.

The nurses strolled past a line of people patiently waiting at a sign *Queue Up Here For Bus*. Their pitifully shabby clothes, rather worn faces, several bandaged arms and legs and heads, bespoke the hardships of war. Yet these English people appeared cheerful and calm. The only betrayal was that the women on line stared at the American girls' nice stockings. Their own were homely makeshifts, much darned.

The girls looked in the window of a food shop. There was little except potatoes, mutton and Brussels sprouts. No eggs, no red meat, no oranges.

Cherry sighed. "Let's go see the church," she suggested.

They went up High Street, past a staid chemist shop which, unlike an American drugstore, was not a wondrous bazaar but sold only drugs, past a stationer's with books in the small window, past the familiar red front of a Woolworth's. They found the church was lovely within, and with the rector's permission, they lingered there.

Coming out, the girls remembered Major Thorne's suggestion that they have a tea party.

"Have we the right to eat these people's limited food?" Ann asked.

They debated it, and decided Major Thorne would not have suggested having tea if it were not all right.

"Besides," Maggie offered shyly, "we'll be careful to eat very, very little."

Cherry remembered having passed a shop with a sign reading *Tiffin at Four O'clock*. She proposed, "Tiffin must mean tea, and four o'clock must mean you can't buy food at any old hour of the day."

They found the shop and went in. It was a modest little tearoom. A plump woman in a flowered apron bustled over to them. She addressed the nurses, in a country accent which they could hardly understand, as "our transatlantic friends." It made Cherry feel very strange to realize she now had the status of a foreigner, albeit a welcome one. The woman apologized that there were no traditional strawberries and thick cream and crumpets for tea during wartime. Instead, she served them excellent tea and paper-thin cucumber sandwiches. They were fun but not filling. Cherry, who had a hearty appetite, began to sympathize in earnest with war-hungered people. Paying for their tiffin led to confusion and hilarity. The big English bank notes looked like wallpaper to them, and the huge coins like lockets. The obliging teashop woman explained, and said as they walked out the door:

"Come back *after* the war. Then you'll see what a jolly country this is!"

The six nurses waited under a great oak for a passing jeep or Army truck.

"We had quite a lark, didn't we," Lieutenant Gray said soberly.

"It was lots of fun," Maggie said in such a subdued voice that they all half-smiled, rather grimly.

"Not much fun, this business of having war in your own front yard," Cherry summed up. She thought gratefully how lucky she was to be an American. She thought too, "It's just as well that I didn't find Mrs. Eldredge this afternoon. I needed to see all this before I could talk with any understanding to any English civilian!"

For the next few days, Cherry helped out in the Army hospital. She met so many new people and was shifted around so much, from ward to X-ray rooms, from giving treatments to soldiers to being circulating nurse at surgeries, that her head whirled. One tired Chief Nurse said to her, "I wish to goodness more of our young girls would enter nursing. There's the free Cadet Nurse Corps scholarship for them, and all. Student nurses, right at home, could relieve this shortage so much, if they only would come forward to help and release older nurses for overseas duty."

"It would mean more American boys' lives saved," Cherry agreed. She knew that, against tremendous odds, the Army and Navy Medical Corps managed to save ninety-six men out of a hundred.

Some extra help did come—from British children, eleven to fifteen years old, who called themselves Cadets. Cherry saw many of these Cadets from the neighborhood around the hospital. United States doctors gave them training. These Cadets proudly did amazingly difficult things—helped take off plaster casts, made plaster bandages, took charge of a desk. Their favorite job was regularly visiting the patients with gifts of food. And how the lonesome GI's enjoyed their visits!

The young Cadets bobbed up with invitations for the nurses from their hospitable parents. Cherry was asked to dinner and to tea almost every day. She was disappointed that, so far, she was far too busy to accept.

And then to her immense delight, Cherry received her first flight order. She was the envy of all Flight Three, for the others' operational orders had not come through yet.

Cherry was on the line at eight A.M., dressed in her blue flying slacks, blouse, and cap—so excited, nervous, and happy she could hardly wait to get started. She waited in a small building—the "base operations"—on the air strip. Bunce, furiously chewing gum, was standing beside her. Like Cherry, he was wearing the white brassard with a Red Cross on his left sleeve. They had already carefully checked to see that straps, seats, and medical kit, were in place for patients. Bunce was too excited to talk. He merely sputtered.

"If I do anything wrong—gosh, Miss Cherry, keep your eyes peeled—maybe you could catch my mistakes in time—"

"You aren't going to make any mistakes, Bunce. Calm down or you'll explode into a million little pieces."

MYSTERY OF MARK GRAINGER 45

"Yes, ma'am! I'm calm! I'm calm like anything! Just—just—I mean—"

"Well, here's our pilot!" Cherry exclaimed.

Captain Cooper strode down the air strip to the base operations hut, past the C-47's with their motors idling. Lieutenants Mason and Greenberg marched together behind him, carrying their gear. Wade was not laughing this morning; he looked almost stern.

"Good morning, Nurse. 'Morning, Sergeant. Parachute checkup. Line up, please."

Cherry nodded hello to the copilot and the radioman as they all lined up and Wade inspected their harness.

"All right, everybody. Destination—Prestwick! Give it everything you've got." Captain Cooper gave orders to his own crew, and to Cherry, "Nurse, whistle when you want me."

"Yes, Captain."

Wade stayed at the hut to make his necessary clearances and manifests—that is, records of crew, weights, weather, flight plan—and to make a last-minute weather check. The flight nurse and her technician walked on ahead to the plane.

At the plane they were joined by the Flight Surgeon, plump little Major Thorne. Then the copilot backed up the C-47 to meet five ambulances rolling down the field. Cherry and Bunce ran, and Major Thorne puffed along too, to be on hand as the ambulance orderlies lifted out the litters.

Cherry caught her breath as she looked into the first litter. She pressed her lips tightly together, to keep from weeping at what she saw. This was no healthy GI playing patient; this was a boy with his leg torn off. In the second litter handed down, lay a khaki-clad fellow whose face was white and set with pain; his tag showed that his spinal cord was severed. "Easy, don't jolt him," she cautioned the stretcher-bearers. She smiled at the lad.

"How are you, fellow?"

"I'm fine, Nurse," he whispered.

In the third litter was a boy in a leather jacket. His shattered jaw was held in place by wires, but his eyes smiled, because he was going home. In the fourth litter was a dazed-looking man. His medical tag read internal wounds and mental shock.

As Cherry bent to look at each casualty, she directed, with the Flight Surgeon's approval, where he should be placed in the plane. Then she hurried off to see that the litters went onto the elevator safely. She found that these skilled medical corpsmen were carrying off the whole loading process with the deftness and silence of a surgical operation. She beckoned to Bunce.

"Sergeant, get up there in the plane with three loaders. Put the broken back in a middle tier where I can reach him easily. Put the internal wounds case way up forward, where the riding is smoother. See if the back case needs a sedative. I have to check in the second ambulance load."

"Yes, ma'am!" Bunce disappeared into the plane.

Cherry returned to the ambulances and the Flight Surgeon. The second ambulance load was gently being lifted out now. After consulting with the Flight Surgeon she hurried back again to the plane. Cherry climbed up into the big transport and stood in the doorway, where she could watch each wounded man as he was lifted in. The litter-bearers sweated and strained under their heavy loads of inert men. They were wonderfully skillful, gentle and patient.

Cherry saw to it that the men were firmly taped in, each on his tier. They seemed to relax, now that they could lie still in one place. She said reassuring words, laid a broken arm in a more comfortable position, and gave a tense soldier an extra smile and pat on the arm. To see a smile come over these wounded men's faces, as she bent over them, was her reward.

In twelve minutes, all eighteen men were loaded and the five ambulances rolled off down the runway. Just before the plane's bay doors were slammed shut, Major Thorne jumped aboard for a last-minute check of the wounded. The Flight Surgeon gave Cherry a few instructions about the spinal and chest cases, then left her in sole charge of the lives of the eighteen men.

Now Cherry looked around for Captain Cooper. He was not in sight.

She found him, not in the base operations hut but not very far away, wistfully poking around a bomber.

"Captain Cooper!" Cherry said furiously. Her black eyes seemed to shoot sparks. "Here is our list of patients!"

They hurried back together to the base operations hut. Wade gloomily reported the list of patients. He and Cherry synchronized their watches. All this went on in heavy silence.

When they got outside, Cherry demanded:

"Wade, what's the matter? What's bothering you?"

"Playing nursemaid! Me!"

"Wade Cooper, this job's every bit as important as piloting a bomber!"

"I know, I know. *More* important. That's just it. I can handle a bomber. I know how to fight. But when I think of eighteen beat-up kids lyin' back there, all helpless, all depending on me—I'm scared cold. Scared and nervous, I tell you."

"Silly, you shouldn't—"

"What altitudes do you want?"

"Keep it as low as you can. We've got a bad chest wound aboard. If you have to go up over eight thousand, give me as much advance notice as you can. Look, you old worrier, there's nothing to be scared of. This is easier than—"

Wade bolted, calling, "Get all belts fastened. Let me know when you're ready back there to take off."

"We're ready now. Won't you come back and tell the boys—"

But Wade was gone. Cherry bit her lip in exasperation.

She tried to reassure the wounded soldiers. Standing in the aisle, she said:

"We have a fine, experienced pilot, fellows. And Sergeant Bunce and I are going to take good care of you. So you just relax and try to sleep."

The weakest men seemed not to have heard. The rest stared back at her solemnly.

Their engines roared. She and Bunce made a final check to see that all the patients were secured. Then they sat down on bucket seats and strapped in. They felt the plane strain, then gently lift. Cherry clasped her hands anxiously. Now came the big test for her—for all of her crew.

Bunce was anxious, too. He whispered to her:

"I put water and coffee and fruit juice in the kitchen. There's plenty of plasma, extra oxygen, and I laid out fresh dressings for that internal wounds case. Oh, yes, and I gave the spinal cord case a sedative. All right?"

"Very all right!" She wished silently that Wade were as thoroughly reliable as Bunce.

They leveled off at around four thousand feet and flew along smoothly in the morning sunlight. Now Cherry had to take back that mental comment. The cockpit door opened and in came the pilot. He walked unsteadily down the aisle between the litters, his eyes glancing into each tier. He faced Cherry sheepishly.

"Copilot took over." Wade cleared his throat. "Uh—everyone comfortable?" Then, without any prompting, he raised his voice and self-consciously said:

"Men, my name's Cooper. I just want you to know that when I was in the ATC, I flew from San Francisco to Stalingrad through a series of storms with a load of machinery and we set her down without a scratch."

Wade said it all in one breath, as if he were ashamed of it.

One weak voice called, "Get any vodka?"

Wade relaxed. "Vodka and champagne and caviar—for breakfast! And they met us at the airport with a brass band!"

There were amused murmurs and smiles along the tiers of wounded men.

"Thanks, Wade," Cherry whispered.

"Sure. Take it easy, fellows!"

Cherry whispered, "I thought you'd flown only in China."

"Well—I—uh—I have to go up forward now. 'Bye." Wade stopped on his way up the crowded aisle to shake a soldier's hand.

"Nice guy," said the patient at Cherry's elbow. He turned his head contentedly and shut his eyes. Cherry could have hugged Wade at that moment.

MYSTERY OF MARK GRAINGER 51

The flight went off smoothly, and the patients (who had already had considerable hospital care) slept most of the way. Subsequent flights went off well, too. Cherry became familiar with the holding hospital at Prestwick, Scotland. Here patients waited six hours or three weeks, to be picked up by transatlantic ATC planes. Four hundred wounded were flown out every morning, westward over the Atlantic, fifteen enormous C-54's at a time. The transfer hospital was a huge barn of a place. "Must be a good deal like lying in Grand Central Station," Wade commented. The men there were cheerful, though, because they were going home. These short hops to Prestwick were easy, Cherry realized. When her team went into combat areas, it would not be so easy as this. Until then, jumping back and forth across the British Isles, eating in strange places, sleeping when and where she could, was a gypsylike existence.

The trips back to home base were carefree. The plane then was empty of patients. They would carry back supplies from ships docking in Scotland, usually medical supplies. Once Cherry was entrusted with a precious package of oral penicillin, which an ATC plane had rushed from New York for a stricken soldier in a British hospital. Cherry thought it would have heartened that soldier's family to see this swift, conscientious aid. On the way back, too, she had a chance to see from aloft the long chain of American Army hospitals scattered throughout England.

Cherry's favorite perch on the way home was beside a low window, back in the fuselage. Lying flat, while floating along in the empty sunshine, she would watch the green hills skim by, listen to the motors' ceaseless throbbing, and dream. Sometimes the sun would sink before they reached home. Then the cabin filled with shadows, while all around and under them, cloud banks piled up, savagely red, swiftly fading.

Sometimes they flew at night. One particular night, an incandescent moon lighted the air. It seemed to Cherry their plane was flying right at the moon. Wade's low voice called her up front. He dismissed his copilot. The silvery-white planet hung just outside the plane's nose.

"Bomber's moon," Wade said to Cherry. "Where is Bunce?"

"Asleep on a litter."

"Want a blanket over your lap?"

"Thanks."

He tucked her in, keeping one hand on the stick. Cherry could see his face in the night light. On his chin there was a streak of red from the dim glow of lights on the instrument panel. Wade smiled at her and his hand touched hers.

"Nice to have a lady aboard."

"Nice to *be* aboard, Captain."

MYSTERY OF MARK GRAINGER   53

"This particular lady, I mean."

"Cooper, Ames, and Company."

"I mean more than that, Cherry."

Then came an event which shattered the smooth-going, easy tenor of these many days and nights.

One afternoon, a mission to Prestwick completed, they circled and prepared to land on their home field. They kept circling. Cherry heard the officers up in front grumbling about something. Lieutenant Greenberg's radio tapped insistently. Finally they did land, easily and smoothly. When Cherry and Bunce flung open the side bays and jumped down, they found the whole field almost deserted. No men, no planes.

Wade shouted from the cockpit, "There's been a bombing! I'm going to taxi the ship over to the hangar. You and Bunce take cover."

Two ground crewmen came running to see if the arriving C-47 was all right. They told Cherry something further.

"Robot bombs. Not aiming for this base—just aiming to destroy anything, kill anybody. One of the villages was hit."

Cherry gasped. "Any civilian wounded in the hospital?"

"Yes—coming in right now—a lot of them."

Cherry and Bunce sprinted across the airfield for the hospital. They saw Army ambulances coming up along the country roads. Redoubling their speed, they burst through the front door, and Cherry started for the second floor where she was assigned.

Captain Betty Ryan caught her on the stairs. "Oh, thank heavens! You got in all right! I've been worrying about you!"

"Yes, ma'am! I'm going to pitch right in!" and Cherry raced on up the stairs. In the corridor she saw dazed-looking English people, women and children and a few old men, some of them badly hurt. She noticed particularly one indignant white-haired lady, a piece of quilt tied over one eye, but her head held high.

The Chief Nurse in charge of the second floor was trying to bring some order into the confusion. Army doctors already were taking care of the severely wounded. Army nurses were trying to classify the walking wounded, according to their injuries, and send them to the right facilities. Cherry was assigned to a cubicle of a room, given supplies, and told to cleanse, medicate, and dress the surface cuts of the people who would be sent in to her. She hastily put on an apron over her flying slacks, and washed, her hands in strong antiseptic. A thirteen-year-old girl Cadet brought a list of names to her, and lined up the patients outside Cherry's door.

"Mr. Thomas Trethaway!" Cherry called.

Into her cubicle came an elderly man. He wore a rusty suit and a blue muffler. His right hand was wrapped in a bloody handkerchief.

"Good day, mum."

"Hello, sir!" Cherry eased off the sticky handkerchief and examined the gaping cut for glass or other particles. "What's happened to that hand?"

"I was just setting meself down to a nice dish o' tea and kippers when—blimey! Jerry drops his calling card. Bits o' the window glass come whirling all over my tea. Kippers aren't easy come by, I can tell you. It was a fair disappointment to me, it was!"

Cherry deftly cleansed and dressed the deep cut. "Well, it may have cost you the kippers, but you're lucky you weren't hurt worse than this."

"I been through worse bombings, *far* worse indeed! But that's nothing. We don't take no notice of that sort of thing."

Mr. Thomas Trethaway calmly took his departure. Cherry called the next name on her list. "Mrs. Ivy Drew!"

In came a frightened young mother with a very young, crying baby. The baby showed no outward signs of injury. Youthful Mrs. Drew said in a trembling voice:

"I found him thrown on the floor. He won't leave off crying, Sister. This time, I thought, 'the Jerries will have had enough of bombing the Drews.' But it seems I was wrong. Can you make him stop crying? Please?"

Cherry took one careful look and saw that the baby had suffered a concussion. She summoned the young Cadet and sent her speeding for a doctor.

"Let's go across the hall, Mrs. Drew," she said gently and led the young mother, with her baby, into a doctor's examining room. Cherry laid the baby down on the table and gave the woman a sedative, to calm her. "Don't you worry. The doctor will take good care of your baby." Talking soothingly, she laid out supplies and instruments which the doctor might need.

The doctor arrived, a little out of breath. "All right, Nurse, thank you."

Cherry returned to her cubicle and treated several more people. Gradually she worked her way down the list. There were only two or three names left. She consulted the list and automatically called out the next name—

"Mrs. Hugh Eldredge!"

—then suddenly recognizing the name, Cherry tensely waited.

The white-haired lady entered. She was quite tall—spare, straight, almost stately, dressed very quietly in black. The taut delicacy of her features and fine faded skin was apparent, despite a large makeshift bandage which completely covered one eye and the side of her face.

"This annoying eye," she murmured. "I daresay it's nothing."

Despite the restrained voice, the elderly woman was quivering. Cherry got her into a chair. Mrs. Eldredge sat defiantly erect. Cherry was bursting with curiosity, but her duty as a nurse came before her personal concerns.

"Now just let me look," Cherry said reassuringly.

The eye was badly bruised, the whole cheek was beginning to discolor, but it was only a surface injury.

"What happened, Mrs. Eldredge?"

"We didn't hear the buzz bomb coming, though the warning had sounded. I went to fetch my little granddaughter from school. On the way—this one was quite near, you see—" Mrs. Eldredge put her hand to her head and sighed.

Cherry gave her a glass of water with a little aromatic spirits of ammonia. When her patient had revived a bit, Cherry asked:

"Is Muriel all right?"

"Yes, thank you. Fortunately Muriel— Why— How did you know my granddaughter's name? She is not here with me!"

"Let me treat that eye first—" Cherry tried to cover her own confusion "—just a moment—"

"How extremely odd! My dear young woman, how did you know that?"

The woman's voice was imperious, and her drawn face was full of distress. Cherry closed the door into the hall. They were quite alone. Cherry said in a low voice:

"I am a friend of your friend in America, Dr. Joseph Fortune."

Mrs. Eldredge gave Cherry such a look of distrust that she was confounded. Mrs. Eldredge made no sign that she had ever heard of Dr. Fortune. "Be discreet," Dr. Joe had warned. Perhaps the woman was waiting for some further token of recognition.

Cherry continued softly, as she bathed the eye, "Dr. Fortune wants me to aid you in your difficulty, in any way you wish me to."

Mrs. Eldredge tossed back her head. "And what would that difficulty be?" she demanded sharply.

"About your son-in-law, Mark Grainger."

Their eyes met.

"Yes. Yes. You know, then."

"No, I know none of the details."

"Tell me your name, my dear."

"Cherry Ames."

"Yes, so Dr. Fortune wrote me. Miss Ames, I—I hope—"

"Yes?"

"Forgive me for being so upset. I have to be so very cautious. Besides, I had hardly expected to meet you under such—rather public circumstances. I do hope you've not spoken of my—trouble—to anyone?"

"To no one."

"When can you come to see me—privately?"

"I can't say exactly. I want to come, Mrs. Eldredge, but we're terribly busy here."

Mrs. Eldredge looked up unhappily at Cherry. All the lines in her face had deepened. "I had better tell you now, then. I promise to keep you but a few moments."

Cherry's dark eyes were wide. Mrs. Eldredge's veined hands plucked nervously at her worn, black silk dress.

"My son-in-law, Mark Grainger," she started, speaking low and rapidly, "is no longer in the Army. He was, and he left." Mrs. Eldredge shook her white head. "I don't understand why he is not fighting for England. But that is not all, Miss Ames. He is always coming and going, without explanation. He will be gone for days, weeks, then return unexpectedly, to leave just as suddenly. I ask him why, where? He will tell me nothing."

"Perhaps he is doing some confidential work," Cherry suggested, chiefly to soothe the elderly woman.

Mrs. Eldredge said with difficulty, "No. That is not so. You see, Miss Ames—one day I was straightening my son-in-law's room and hanging away his clothing, when a bit of paper fell from one of his pockets. It was—this is very hard to say—it was a note in German, on paper of a sort one never sees in England! The handwriting was that stiff German script, you know, not an English person's writing. I was trying to figure out what it said when Mark came in. He snatched the paper away—he is never rude—and he was exceedingly angry!"

Cherry did not know exactly what to say to this. "But your son-in-law is—is loyal to his own country, surely?"

The woman bent her head. "I don't know. That is just the question. I used to think Mark was loyal. It is hard to believe the husband of one's own daughter—Lucia was killed by the enemy—could—Oh, no! It's unthinkable!"

Cherry sat down beside the elderly lady and took her hand. "Perhaps it's only a mistake—a coincidence—or you're imagining something."

"No! I have gone to the telephone and had strange voices address me in German. When I reply, they immediately hang up. I have heard Mark admitting people into my house in the dead of night. No, Miss Ames, I am not imagining these things." Suddenly she cried out in a subdued but sharp voice, "How could he? How could he? I'm so confused. I want to trust Lucia's husband—if only for Muriel's sake—but how can I be loyal to my son-in-law and disloyal to my country?"

Cherry thought a moment. "Does Muriel suspect?"

"The poor child is very much troubled. You see, the neighbors are wondering. They ask her cruel questions. She adores her father. I often ask myself how to protect her from such—such a—"

Cherry cut in quickly. "Surely he would not betray his own little girl? But your son-in-law gives no explanations at all?" she asked.

"None. He simply turns a deaf ear to all questions. Oh, Miss Ames, I've not told a soul but you! I—I am heartsick!"

Cherry's lips silently formed the word that Mrs. Eldredge could not bring herself to say:

"Spy!"

She took a deep breath. "Mrs. Eldredge, you must go home now and rest. The ambulance will drive you back. I will come to see you on my very first free moment. For the little girl's sake," she added, "perhaps we will find some way out of this."

The white-haired lady rose wearily. "You have been very kind, my dear. I shall be waiting for you." She walked out, head high.

Spy … The word echoed in Cherry's mind. What sort of man was this Mark Grainger? Yet the little girl adored him, the grandmother had claimed, and children were extremely sensitive to grownup's wrongdoings. She could not reconcile these two facts. But Cherry did not doubt the truth of Mrs. Eldredge's reports, either. One did not breathe such accusations against a member of one's own family unless they were inescapably true. Certainly there was not much to be said in defense of such a man. And yet if the child still loved him—

"Somehow I'm not convinced that he is a spy," Cherry thought. "Until I can find out more, I'll take my stand with little Muriel!"

In the meantime, she had her work, with Wade and Bunce and Flight Three, to do.

CHAPTER IV

"Aunt" Cherry

THREE TIMES IT HAPPENED. CHERRY WENT DOWN TO THE line, all packed to take off, keyed up, all ready—and then they could not go out because of bad weather. All flight orders were canceled—three times in succession.

It was exasperating. Cherry worried over the patients who had to wait. As for herself, she felt at loose ends and restless. So did everyone else. But there was plenty to take up the nurses' time. There was hospital duty, washing of clothes and catching up on rest—blessed, needed rest—for the next flight. It was the first time that all of Flight Three was at home at the same time. The six girls had a chance to visit, and it looked as if Lieutenant Agnes Gray was finally going to achieve a foursome for a bridge game.

"I don't care how badly you play," Aggie pleaded. The Flight Three nurses were sitting and lying around their barracks room, this rainy fall morning, weathered-in. Even drill had been canceled. Everyone was waiting around to see if the skies would clear. "I would give my eyeteeth for a rubber of bridge. Cherry, what about you?"

Cherry was prone on her bed. She reluctantly opened her black eyes, and rubbed one stockinged foot against the other. "If I can play lying down, okay. Seems to me I *never* get rested."

"Me too," said big Elsie Wiegand from her bed.

Gwen, her red head buried in the depths of her pillow, mumbled agreement.

"Ann? Maggie?" Agnes pleaded. "We could leave out these frail flowers and play three-handed."

"*Not* frail flowers," Cherry yawned. "Just had heavier schedules than you."

Little Maggie turned around innocently from the washbasin. "If you'll wait till I finish my washing, I'll play—if you'll teach me."

Ann emerged from the depths of her foot locker. "I'll play but it has to be for safety pins. I am absolutely desperate for safety pins."

Agnes Gray flung out her arms. "All right, no bridge! But I have to *do* something!" Her reddish brown eyes snapped. She reminded Cherry of a fox terrier, bursting with energy. "What'll I *do* with myself?"

"Find me some safety pins," Ann replied promptly.

"That's no fun!"

Cherry propped herself up on one elbow, wound and rewound one jet black curl around her finger. "I—think—I—have an idea."

"Watch out, kids," Gwen said. "Ames is having an idea. Stand back to avoid the explosion."

"Maybe we could—how's this sound? Maybe we could set up a barter system," Cherry thought out loud. "Have to get poor little Annie her safety pins. Yes, a barter system. In this whole barracks. Let's see, two squadrons—fifty girls—safety pins—that's it, that's it!" She sat up excitedly. "Don't you see?"

"No!" they chorused. "See *what*?"

"Look, I'll show you!" Cherry forgot her fatigue, and bounced off her bed. "Aggie and Ann, we'll start with you. Who'll come with me to knock on doors?"

Two hours later, the system was organized and in full swing. Instead of money, candy and bobby pins were the medium of exchange and estimating price. One girl in Flight Two, with a sweet tooth, offered a finger wave in return for chocolate bars—"with almonds," she stipulated. Ann wangled safety pins in exchange for a piece of clothesline and a bar of soap. Gwen, who could fix almost anything mechanical with pliers and her tweezers, agreed to repair watches, loosen balky luggage locks, and untie knots—if the other girl would do Gwen's ironing, a chore Gwen detested. Another nurse agreed to mend hose in exchange for two shoeshines. Elsie Wiegand rented her typewriter for writing V-mails

"AUNT" CHERRY 65

at a charge of starch for her shirt collars. Cherry needed face powder—she had spilled most of hers. But Cherry was too busy getting all this organized to do any bartering herself at the moment. Every nurse in the barracks had fun and everyone benefited. Aggie Gray, the last Cherry saw of her, was beaming at three unknown nurses across a bridge game. The only things the nurses did not swap were their pilots, although they discussed even that possibility.

The weather continued stormy. During a lull, flight orders were issued, then had to be canceled again. Planes were grounded. Cherry wished she could have some time off, to visit Mrs. Eldredge and Muriel, instead of just waiting around. But Captain Betty Ryan, though willing personally, was under orders not to give time off to any nurse.

Finally Cherry wrote: "Dear Mrs. Eldredge, It is impossible for me to leave the base. However, I have free time just now. Would it be asking too much for you to come here, any day, for lunch or dinner in Officers' Mess? I'd be so glad to see you. Please tell Muriel she is very particularly invited. Sincerely, Cherry Ames, Nurses' Barracks C."

But there was no answer next day, nor the following day. Cherry grew even more restive, wondering if something had happened to Mrs. Eldredge and Muriel. At least the weather was clearing now. A few combat planes went out.

"I've received a flight order," Ann told Cherry breathlessly in their quarters. "Thank goodness! I'm going out in an hour."

Elsie Wiegand burst in. "Praise be, some action, at last! I'm going out at twelve midnight. Any orders for you, Cherry?"

Cherry shook her head. "Nothing yet."

She helped the two girls pack. She helped out on wards at the hospital. She listened to the bombers and fighters going out, haunted by their fading roar, not quite easy until, hours later, they roared home again. She and Wade knew the boys flying those planes—Bob and Ducky, Shep and Al and Tiny. Toward evening, she would stand out on the field with Wade, anxiously counting the bombers and fighters that flew in singly, some limping like wounded birds, some triumphantly roaring down from the skies. Too often, Cherry's count was short—one, two, three planes and their crews had not returned. Sometimes until midnight Cherry and Wade would wait on the cold blacked-out field with the anxious ground crewmen, scanning the skies, their ears alert for any distant sound of familiar engines. More often than she dared hope, a belated crew would come pounding in, sometimes radioing for an ambulance, sometimes kidding and hungry. Or, after she was in bed, she would hear a plane's roar in the night, and Wade would tell her at breakfast, "Shep and his boys made it! Boy, what I'd have given to have been along!"

"Quite some lads," Cherry would reply. "I'm glad I'm here."

This was her way of saying that the fliers' courage renewed her own idealism. She was proud to be helping such men as these.

One doubt invariably filtered into her deeply felt bond with these men. Of what avail was these mens' courage, their hard fighting, the deaths of some of them—if there were a spy in their midst? Suppose some spy—Cherry did not want to name him as Mark Grainger—suppose some spy were reporting to the Germans all the flights and plans of this bomber base? The enemy, forewarned, could bring their plans to nothing.

Cherry wanted very much to talk about this with Wade. Captain Cooper, for all his lighthearted fooling, had a level head and much experience. For the present, though, she had promised Mrs. Eldredge to guard her confidences.

One morning Cherry found the awaited letter in her mail. It was on rustling, square white paper, written in a fine old-fashioned hand: "Dear Miss Ames, I regret that a severe cold prevents my accepting your kind invitation to luncheon or dinner at your Officers' Mess. However, Muriel is most eager to come, to meet you and to sit at table with the American nurses. A neighbor, Mrs. Jaynes, will deliver Muriel to your barracks today at eleven-thirty, which should be in adequate time for luncheon. If you will advise Mrs. Jaynes at what hour luncheon is over, she will bring Muriel home then. With thanks, Frances Eldredge (Mrs. Hugh Eldredge)."

Cherry delightedly said to the other nurses, "Today, I'm going to have a guest, aged six years old!"

Promptly at eleven-thirty a knock sounded on Cherry's door. She answered and found a smiling woman in knickers. A small girl was hiding behind her.

"I'm Mrs. Jaynes," the woman said. "Muriel and I have cycled up. Muriel? Are you there? Don't be so shy, dear."

She drew forward a mite of a girl. Soft, fair hair shadowed the child's enormous eyes. Her little face was like a serious elf's.

"Say how-do-you-do to Lieutenant Ames, dear."

Muriel obediently opened her small pink mouth but no sound came out. She was staring at Cherry with frightened, fascinated eyes.

"Hello, Muriel," Cherry said smiling. "I'm very glad you came."

The child dropped her eyelids. Lashes long as a doll's brushed her pale cheeks. She held on tightly to a miniature, worn leather purse. Cherry saw how worn her little dark blue woolen suit was, too short at the tiny chiseled wrists, and how thin the child was under those garments. The tenseness of the little figure, the pinched face, were pitiful signs that Muriel had spent all her brief life under the strain of war.

The little girl stared at the floor. Then she glanced up fleetingly and put her hand in Cherry's, and left it there.

"Mrs. Jaynes," Cherry said, "I'm expecting you to lunch too."

"Thank you, but no." The neighbor explained that she had other errands to do, in another village, and would call for Muriel in an hour or two or three.

Muriel unexpectedly spoke up, shyly but clearly. Her English accent was less an accent than a certain primness of inflection. "Please don't come for me too soon, Mrs. Jaynes."

Both Cherry and Mrs. Jaynes laughed. They arranged for Cherry to telephone her—"ring her up"—in another village, when it was time for Muriel to leave. The neighbor said good-bye.

"Did you ride on the handle bars?" Cherry asked, leading the little girl into her room. She had already shooed out the other nurses.

Muriel still would not look at her. "No. In the parcel basket behind. Grandmother wishes to be remembered to you." She fumbled for a long time in her big pocket, and dug out something wrapped in a clean handkerchief. "This is for you, from the fruiterer's."

"Why, thank you!" It was an apple, lovingly polished till it shone. Cherry sniffed it, admired it. "We'll split it. You'll eat half and I'll eat half."

For the first time, a ghost of a smile formed on the pale little face. "*After* luncheon, of course," Muriel said solemnly.

"Let's sit down," Cherry suggested. The two girls, one big and one little, sat down side by side on one of the beds. Muriel carefully smoothed her skirt. She glanced up at Cherry with those enormous haunted eyes, and gradually she smiled, a real smile this time.

"Why is this place tinted violet? Are there any other children here? I never knew any Americans before, you know. Why did your mother name you Cherry?"

Cherry hastened to keep pace with Muriel's questions. But Muriel prattled on.

"My mother's name was Lucia. She's dead. The Jerries killed her. She's beautiful in her picture. I have a dog, though. A jolly brown dog named Lilac. My father says Lilac—" The child stopped. Her brows drew together. Cherry wondered whether she were looking so troubled about Lilac or about her father.

"Will we have a sweet at luncheon? I'm frightfully tired of porridge all the time," the piping voice went on. "You see, Lilac and Grandmother and I, we all eat porridge. Lilac doesn't like porridge a bit better than I do."

"I don't like oatmeal much myself. You shall have dessert at lunch and some chocolate to take home," Cherry promised.

"AUNT" CHERRY

"Chocolate," Muriel breathed. "My father brought it to me sometimes. Is luncheon served presently?"

"Immediately! Let's walk over."

"Right-o."

The walk over to Officers' Mess was virtually a triumphal parade of two. The other nurses oh'd and ah'd when they saw Cherry's small visitor. The pilots were no less smitten by this grave elf of a girl. At the long table, surrounded by grownups, Muriel was so smothered with attentions that she was bewildered. Gwen, across the table, gave her, her pat of butter and her pickles. Dick Greenberg hunted up a glass of milk with—bliss!—chocolate syrup in it. Wade left his chair on Muriel's other side and canvassed the room, frankly asking nurses and pilots to contribute some of their cookies. Even Major Thorne came over, plump and beaming, to shake Muriel's small hand and present her with a package of chewing gum. She was overwhelmed, unable to say anything to anybody beyond whispered thank-you's.

"Now you must eat," Cherry said in a low voice. She drew Muriel's chair closer to her own and cut up her lamb for her. Muriel leaned over to Cherry.

"When may I chew the gum?"

"After lunch. Come now, this is awfully good—"

Muriel automatically opened her mouth, chewed, swallowed hastily, and leaned close again to whisper, "Please, is Captain Cooper your friend? I do like *him*.

Only why do Americans hold their forks in the wrong hand?"

Cherry explained and urged her to eat. After protesting she was not hungry, Muriel settled down and finished her portion, including a nibble off Cherry's plate, and a taste of Wade's coffee, and Wade's, Maggie's and Gwen's jello. She looked profoundly happy and sleepy.

"Want to take a nap?" Cherry asked.

"Oh, no! I wouldn't waste a minute! This is fun no end!"

She trotted along at Cherry's side, lugging Wade's cookies, the chewing gum, her purse and a handful of lump sugar "for Lilac." Bill Mason's Pacific theater ribbon was pinned conspicuously on her jacket. She and Cherry walked as far as the lounge of Officers' Mess, when a delegation of nurses met them.

"Halt!" said Gwen, holding up her hand. "Lieutenant Cherry, we have conferred, and decided that Miss Muriel Grainger should not be your guest alone. Our whole squadron would like to invite her to be—ahem!—our mascot! Major Thorne has given his permission."

The little girl edged closer to Cherry and clung to her jacket.

Cherry bent down and whispered, "Would you like that?"

"What *is* a mascot?" Muriel whispered back. "What does a mascot have to do?"

Cherry explained this, too. "It's a great compliment, and lots of fun."

Muriel whispered, "Please tell them, yes, thank you."

"Don't you want to tell them yourself?"

But this was beyond the six-year-old's courage. As Cherry accepted for her, she stared solemnly at the nurses, a little flush of color in her cheeks.

There was an outburst of applause, there in the foyer. Muriel dodged behind a chair. Her reticent expression said clearly that these hearty Americans were too much for her. But when Cherry fished her out, she was smiling.

Muriel's shyness gradually wore off on her subsequent visits to the base. Cherry had arranged for the child to come over with Mrs. Jaynes, during the lull between flights. The nurses had, she explained to Mrs. Eldredge in another note, to make their mascot a uniform.

Making a flight nurse's uniform in size six was quite a problem. Maggie owned the smallest slate-blue jacket they could find. Cutting it down yielded a small-size jacket and a miniature pair of slacks for the mascot. The girls fitted these to her with precise military tailoring, while small Muriel stood so still she scarcely breathed. The big brass buttons for the front of the jacket looked enormous on Muriel. Cherry found, however, that the smaller buttons from cuffs and pockets were just right. Maggie and Ann, who were the nimblest with needles, did most of this work. Agnes Gray cut down one of her trench caps to perch on the small fair head. Cherry got Wade to drive her into the villages, where she hunted in the modest shops for a boy's military-looking shirt. Wade contributed a regulation tie, from which Muriel acquired three ties, and he insisted on buying a little shoulder-strap bag.

All this took several days, and several thrilled visits on the mascot's part. Some of the girls were absent now and then on flights, but fortunately, Cherry had received no flight order as yet. At last the tiny uniform was completed, even to the lieutenant's bar.

Cherry, Ann, little Maggie and Agnes Gray dressed the six-year-old in her blue jacket and slacks. They cocked the trench cap to the right, at the precise angle. In the little shoulder-strap bag, Cherry put peanuts, a handkerchief and two shiny new American dimes. Muriel stood there pale with excitement, and very, very proud.

"Well!" said Cherry, lifting Muriel to the mirror. "It isn't every six-year-old who enters the Army as a full-fledged lieutenant!"

"What's more," Agnes pointed out, "Muriel probably is the first little English girl ever to wear an American flight nurse's uniform."

Cherry set Muriel down again. Other nurses in the barracks came filtering in to see the new mascot. Muriel tugged at Cherry's sleeve. "Please teach me to salute?"

"AUNT" CHERRY

So they taught her to salute. She practiced patiently, until the nurses pronounced her salute "Snappy!"

She sat down happily on Cherry's lap, beamed, and dangled her legs. She was still too shy to answer all the questions of the nurses. Suddenly she piped up:

"You're all my aunts! I just figured it out!"

The girls laughed. "Of course, that's right!" "Muriel's American aunts!" "Everyone knows a mascot has to have an aunt!"

Muriel fished in her bag and proudly passed around her precious peanuts and chewing gum. Oddly enough, none of the aunts seemed to wish any peanuts or gum at just that moment. Cherry, under Muriel's pleading, did take one peanut—which they shared.

"Mm, delicious! Now, please, may we go for a walk?" The small-size flight nurse breathed to Cherry, "Maybe to show Captain Wade my uniform!"

They found Wade poking around their grounded C-47. Wade registered amazement at the tiny figure in flight nurse's slacks, walking so erect and proudly at Cherry's side.

"Who could this be? A new nurse for our crew? Lieutenant Grainger, my compliments!" Wade came smartly to attention, clicked his heels, and flung out his hand in salute.

Muriel immediately answered with a snappy salute. Then she dimpled. "It's only I, Captain Wade. Not a real nurse."

"Well, you certainly had me fooled!" Wade strolled over and hoisted the miniature nurse to his shoulder. "I could do that with you, too, Lieutenant Ames. Want to see the plane, cherub?"

Muriel was rapturous as Wade lifted her into the cockpit and let her finger the controls "that make the plane fly." She wandered wide-eyed through the big cabin, tried sitting on several bucket seats, and begged Cherry to paint her fingernails red, like the nurses, with the red mercurochrome she spied in the medical kit. Cherry obliged. She was sorry Bunce was not here, too, to enjoy this.

"What goes bang-bang at the Jerries?" the elf in slacks wanted to know, waving her tinted fingers.

"No guns aboard, cherub," said Wade.

"Oh. Well, then, if Cherry is my aunt, are you my uncle?"

Wade's laughing brown eyes turned gleefully to Cherry. She felt herself flushing.

"Could be, Lieutenant Grainger, could be. A very smart question. Ask us again from time to time, will you?"

"'Course."

Cherry sputtered, and then she and Wade burst out laughing.

Little Muriel studied them patiently. "What's funny? I don't think it's funny. It's nice. Cherry is my favorite aunt."

"AUNT" CHERRY

Wade, looking at Cherry with softened eyes, assured her, "Cherry is my favorite, too. Now isn't that a coincidence? Let's go get you some refreshments. All small fry should be stuffed with refreshments!"

He lifted the small nurse and then helped the grown-up nurse down from the open bays to the ground.

"I'm not small fried—I'm not fried at all!" Muriel protested.

"Want a ride in a chair?" Wade motioned to Cherry. They clasped their hands around each other's wrists, making a chair for the six-year-old. She rode off between her flying "aunt and uncle" wearing an expression of sheer bliss.

That night after lights were out in Nurses' Barracks C, Cherry could not sleep for thinking about their little mascot—and Mark Grainger. Cherry had lost her heart to this sad-eyed child who had known only war, and Cherry was only a friend. How much more must a parent love her! Then how could Mark Grainger do anything to jeopardize his little girl's safety, or submit her to cruel gossip among the neighbors? Cherry turned uneasily under the khaki blankets. She tried to recall what Muriel had said about her father. Nothing, so far. The nurses had kept her so busy, the youngster had had no chance to prattle of her own accord. She was too reticent, besides, to confide much to any brand-new friends. Perhaps later ... perhaps on a visit to Mrs. Eldredge's house ... Cherry drifted off to sleep.

The drizzling rains ceased and the mists lifted a little. Cherry and Wade began again to carry the wounded to Prestwick. It was now nearing the end of November, but Cherry waited in vain for snow or crisp cold in England. It was nearing Thanksgiving, too, she thought nostalgically.

She managed to have a little private visit with Bunce on Thanksgiving Day. Nurses, being officers, were not supposed to fraternize with enlisted men, but Cherry—an old Army girl by now—had learned that the American Army is a friendly one. So she and her old friend and sergeant met Thanksgiving morning, after church service, to take a walk down one of the country lanes.

"I'm so homesick," young Bunce confided, "I could break down and blubber. Gosh, I'd like to see my mother! And our house, and my two kid brothers, and my town. This war, Miss Cherry, is an awful lonesome war.

"It sure is. Well, Bunce, whenever you get so lonesome you can't stand it, you just come and tell me about it."

Bunce grinned down at her from his lanky six feet. His candid blue eyes and tousled hair might better have been atop a small boy, than such a tall man. He gave a vigorous chew on his gum, hesitated a moment, and then said earnestly:

"Miss Cherry, 'scuse me for askin', but what's on your mind lately? Seems to me you're thinkin' awful hard about something. Is it that little girl?"

Cherry glanced up at him, startled. "Well—uh— Don't take such long strides, Bunce. Yes, I have been worrying about that youngster."

"War orphan, I guess."

"In a way." Cherry let it go at that, and Bunce seemed satisfied. She would have liked to take Bunce into her confidence, for she knew from past experience how helpful he could be. But she knew she must keep the story of Mark Grainger to herself.

"Bunce," she asked, "did I tell you that Muriel is coming over for dinner today?"

Bunce kicked along some pebbles in the road. "Miss Cherry, 't'ain't fair. Why just one little girl? There're dozens of youngsters in the neighborhood who need us for aunts and uncles too. Why couldn't we adopt a whole bunch of 'em?"

"That's an idea! Maybe a Christmas party for all the children for miles around!"

"Aw, shucks, a whole month to wait?"

Cherry smiled. "The woman who runs our barracks has two little boys—if you insist on sharing your Thanksgiving dinner!"

The young guests hugely enjoyed their first Thanksgiving dinner. Muriel's share of turkey and candied sweet potatoes and cranberry sauce impressed her very much. Perched on a chair and three thick books, she absorbed food and the noble story of Thanksgiving with equal seriousness.

Late that afternoon, Cherry and Wade took her home. Cherry and her pilot had the rest of the evening off. Wade bundled "my two girls" into the front seat of a borrowed jeep, tossed a blanket over their laps, and squeezed in behind the wheel. As usual, he drove on two wheels, and sang in a booming baritone:

"One—meat—BALL! Now ain't that sad—on-ly ONE meat BALL!"

Cherry giggled as much as small Muriel did. "Don't you know any other song?" she demanded.

"Nope. Don't need to. *One Meat Ball* is a fine song. Suits me. You know any songs, cherub?"

Muriel knitted her brows. "I know about Mother Goose. But I guess you heard those. I know one my father taught me, last time he came home."

She started to sing in a thin, earnest, tuneless chant. The words were in German. Wade glanced at Cherry over the little fair head. Cherry uncomfortably looked straight ahead at the road.

When Muriel finished the song, Wade said that was "real fine," only he and Cherry couldn't understand the words. What was the song about?

Muriel said, "My father told me, but I forget. Some thing about *Röslein*, roses and a girl. Not English roses, not a girl here in England, though. Anyhow, I like the Meat Ball song better! You know what, Captain Wade?" she prattled along. "You know much better songs than my father. Of course I love my father very very much," she explained seriously, "more than anyone in the world. Whenever he comes home, we have such fun together. Lilac too."

Cherry heard this speech with growing uneasiness. She wanted to ask questions, yet in decency she could not question a child. She did not want to discuss the child's doubtful father before anyone else, either. Wade certainly was looking puzzled and on the alert.

"Your daddy in the British Army?"

"He used to be."

Wade glanced again at Cherry. Then, to her relief, he said in his usual lighthearted way, "Well, cherub, I'm no linguist but I could teach you pig Latin. Now, you take the first letter of a word, and put it at the end, like this—Uriel-may. That's your name. Surprised?"

Muriel promptly replied, "I-ay already-ay ow-knay ig-pay atin-Lay!"

Wade looked so astonished, so thunderstruck, that all three of them laughed the rest of the way into the village.

Muriel importantly directed Wade past the pub on High Street and to the right down a quiet lane. At last the jeep drew up before a regular storybook house.

It was a low, rambling cottage, white with blue shutters, and a blue door. Hedges and bare flower beds surrounded it, damply fragrant in the misty twilight. Branches of low, old trees brushed the windows. Cherry would not have been surprised if Queen Mab and her "faëry ring," or Puck himself, had come tumbling down the wet eaves on a breath of air.

"This is where I live!" the tiny flight nurse announced. "Please, both of you, come in for tea. Grandmother said I was to ask you."

Cherry and Wade heard only absent-mindedly: they were under the spell of this place.

"Please come in?"

The two Americans roused themselves. Wade said to Cherry, "I'll come to the door and be properly introduced to the cherub's grandmother. But, gosh, don't make me sit around at a ladies' tea party. I'll meet some of the fellows at the inn and I'll drive back here for you around eight or nine. All right? Besides," he added shrewdly, "you may have something private to talk over with the cherub's grandmother."

The blue door opened and Mrs. Eldredge stood in the doorway, on the single stone step. She was a tall, valiant white-haired figure with the lamplight shining out behind her.

"Do come in!" she called in her clipped British voice. "So nice of you to trouble with Muriel."

"AUNT" CHERRY

Muriel held open the gate. They went up the path. Wade looked very brown, very young, very American, next to this parchment-like lady as Cherry said, "Mrs. Eldredge, Captain Cooper."

"Delighted, Captain."

"How do you do!"

Wade made his excuses and, after whispering to the disappointed little girl, climbed back into the jeep and drove away.

"Come in, my dear."

Cherry followed her dignified hostess into the living room—or sitting room, as the English called it. It was a low, square, wall-papered room, dominated by a brick fireplace, and cozily furnished. There were pictures and books and a sewing basket. The room looked so unassuming and homelike that it took Cherry a few moments to realize these comfortable mahogany armchairs, the stately sideboard with its sprigged porcelain dishes, the wing chair of faded needlepoint, the flowery waxy chintz curtains, were all very beautiful things. A framed photograph of a young man caught her eye.

Mrs. Eldredge smiled at Cherry's frank curiosity, but said nothing.

Cherry burst out with honest admiration, "I've seldom seen anything so inviting!"

"War has left it all sadly worn and in need of repair. Would you like to see the other rooms?"

"Oh, may I?"

Muriel interrupted, romping in with a shaggy brown nondescript dog nearly as big as she was.

"This is Lilac!" she announced. "Isn't he beautiful?"

"He's very nice," Cherry chuckled and patted the floppy ears. Lilac sniffed hard, wagged his tail, barked, offered his clumsy paw, rolled over, and ended up by noisily licking Cherry's hand.

"Isn't he smart!" his small owner beamed. "He's part collie, part Airedale, and part I-don't-know-what-else."

Cherry, Muriel, and the overgrown puppy made up a retinue, following Mrs. Eldredge through the house. There were three oak-beamed bedrooms with high-backed wooden beds and plump goose-down comfortables, patched it was true but still tempting. There was a roomy old-fashioned kitchen which Mrs. Eldredge called the scullery, a laundry room, and a bathroom whose brassy fixtures were fancy, old and inconvenient. In fact, everything in the house, from its uneven bare wooden floors to the last teaspoon, was worn threadbare. Yet everything gleamed with good care and with honest use.

They returned to the living room and sat by the smoldering wood fire. Mrs. Eldredge talked interestingly of old houses. Cherry could not keep her lively dark eyes from straying to the framed photograph on the mantel.

"That is my son-in-law. Muriel dear, bring Miss Ames the picture."

"AUNT" CHERRY

Cherry held the photograph and studied it. The man, just past first youth, was handsome and of fair coloring. The features were strong, clear-cut, well proportioned; the mouth was firm. Cherry could see in Muriel's baby face a likeness to that rather long head, that high, finely molded forehead.

"That portrait was made just after Mark left the Army. An odd occasion to have one's picture taken," Mrs. Eldredge added bitterly.

Muriel's little face was filled with distress. She took the picture from Cherry and clasped it to her, as if to defend her father.

Cherry was appalled to see defiant tears in the child's eyes. "Poor little sprite!" she thought.

Mrs. Eldredge sighed. "You have a picture of your mother, too, dear."

"Oh, yes, Aunt Cherry! Want to see it?"

After lovingly setting down her father's picture, Muriel trotted out. She returned carrying a little leather folder. Cherry found herself looking into a lovely young face, with Muriel's same enormous, sensitive eyes. A cascade of golden hair fell about the lovely Lucia's throat.

"Isn't my mother beautiful? I love her dearly."

Mrs. Eldredge said quietly, "That is the only mother Muriel has—a bit of paper—and I have no daughter—thanks to the Germans." She looked down at her veined hands. "Muriel does not remember her mother.

Unfortunately she scarcely sees her father. Her father—Mark is—Are you ready for tea? Shall we have our tea now?" She nervously got busy.

There was nothing Cherry could say. She assisted her elderly hostess in bringing in dishes and food, determined to make herself a cheerful guest in this brave house. She expressed her surprise that tea could be a real supper—though Cherry guessed that her hostess had spread out most of her rations for a whole week, to be hospitable. Muriel's widened eyes proved that.

"Do have some more, Miss Ames," urged Mrs. Eldredge.

But Cherry was careful not to accept too much.

The trio grew quite gay over this feast. Mrs. Eldredge told Cherry the history of the curious cups her deceased husband had brought from India, and showed her beautiful Paisley shawls.

They were folding the big shawls when the outer door opened and Mark Grainger came in.

For a second there was tense silence. Cherry saw Mrs. Eldredge stiffen. Then Muriel, whose mouth was open in surprise, gave a whoop of delight and ran into her father's arms.

He picked her up, held her high, their two fair heads close, and demanded, "How is my daughter today? And what is this you are wearing?"

"My uniform—I'm a mascot now. Extremely well, thank you. How are you? Oh, father I didn't know you were coming home!"

"I didn't know it myself." Mark Grainger kissed her and gently put her down. Then he went over to the grandmother. "How are you, Mother Eldredge? Are you all right? How is the head?"

"Improving, thank you." The elderly woman hesitated, then met his eyes and forced a smile. "Well, Mark! Quite a surprise. We're happy to have you at home. Let me present you to an American friend of Dr. Fortune's—Lieutenant Cherry Ames."

Cherry shook hands with Mark Grainger. She took a good look at this man. He was about twenty-seven or eight, a little above medium height, dressed unobtrusively in a dark gray suit. He seemed weary, but otherwise he gave an impression of great vigor and character.

Cherry said she would take her departure now. But they all insisted she stay, and settled down for a visit.

"I dare say you're famished, Mark. Tea is already on the table."

"I am half starved. Literally." But he did not say why, or where he had been, or how he had happened to arrive so unexpectedly. Cherry saw that Mrs. Eldredge, even Muriel, tensely avoided asking any questions. There was a kind of dread in the old lady's saddened eyes. Yet—remarkably—Mark Grainger sat at the table, eating, completely at ease, completely happy and at home here. Was he callous, cynical—or did he have a clear conscience despite the silent accusation in this room?

"May I stay up late, very late?" Muriel begged.

"You may stay up a bit longer, to see your father. Mark, Miss Ames has been exceptionally kind to Muriel. She has been entertaining her at the American installation."

Mark's eyes lit up. "I am most grateful to you. I'm sure you are supplying most of the happiness in her life just now." There was a tone of deep regret in his voice. Then he gave her a friendly smile. "You're a flight nurse, aren't you, Miss Ames?"

"Yes, Mr. Grainger."

"I'm an engineer. I've been in the Army and I've also done some engineering work for the British government." It sounded very smooth and plausible, the way he said it. He deftly turned the subject away from his activities. "It was while I was studying engineering in your country that I had the great pleasure of knowing Dr. Fortune. How is he—and what is he doing now?"

Cherry replied, not too specifically, that Dr. Fortune was doing some sort of medical work for the American Army.

"Research, I suppose?" Mark said pleasantly.

"I'm not sure, Mr. Grainger."

"Dr. Fortune's passion was research when *I* knew him. A remarkable man. Lucia was very fond of him."

Cherry was puzzled. How could this man probe for information for the enemy—if that was what he was doing—yet in the next breath, mention his wife whom the enemy had killed? Or was this only the most innocent of conversations? It could be interpreted either way.

Muriel was having a fine time sitting on her father's knee and telling him about her adventures as mascot. "I'm going to go up in the plane!" she invented. "And fly all over, and help win the war! Did you ever go up in a plane?"

Mark smiled. "Sometimes, yes."

Cherry pricked up her ears. What sort of plane? Going where?

Then he added quickly, "Before the war, I often flew to various jobs. That's before you were here, Muriel."

"But do you ride in planes *now*?" the little girl insisted.

Her young father hesitated. "Let's talk of something else."

Mrs. Eldredge interposed dryly, "Yes, let us, indeed!"

Cherry waited for Mark's reply. But he made no move to defend himself. He asked Muriel in a low voice, "Do those naughty children still call you names?"

"It's only on *your* account that they taunt her!" Mrs. Eldredge said sharply.

Still Mark Grainger made no explanations. His face tightened momentarily: that was all.

The rest of his visit belonged to Muriel, with due attention for Lilac. There were fairy tales, conversation, conundrums, and a good romp around the living room. Muriel glowed with happiness; her handsome young father looked every bit as happy, and deeply moved. Cherry thought, "Even evil men might love their own children." Yet, there was something so forthright in this man's face—something so pleasant in his strong voice—Or was it simply good acting?

A knock sounded, and the door opened a second time. There stood an old man of the neighborhood. When he saw Mark, a dour look spread over his weather beaten face.

"Come in, Mr. Heath!" Mrs. Eldredge said. "Will you have a cup of tea? It's so damp tonight—"

But Mr. Heath hung back, standing gingerly at the threshold as if the visitor might contaminate him.

"I just come to say good evening and tell you Mrs. Heath sends her thanks for the periodicals." He threw a bitter look at Mark, then glanced at Muriel. "Poor little 'un."

Just then the phone rang. It was an old-fashioned phone on the wall. Mrs. Eldredge rose and answered it. She listened, then bent her head. "It's for you, Mark."

He sprang up, suddenly charged into action and impersonality. "Yes ... Yes—Speak louder—Very good, immediately."

The young man seized his coat and like a whirlwind, kissed Muriel, called, "Good-bye, Mother! Good-bye, Miss Ames! Please take care of Muriel"—and all but ran out the door.

Mr. Heath, who had taken all this in, picked up a cushion Mark had knocked to the floor in his hurry. "Good night, mum. I don't think I'll be staying." The old neighbor closed the blue door emphatically behind him.

Mrs. Eldredge sat down and put her hand over her eyes. The room, so lively a moment before, was now so quiet Cherry could hear the clock ticking and the leaves rustling outside.

Cherry sat down, too, and took Muriel on her lap. She was determined to protect this bewildered child, as much as anyone could, from her grandmother's bitterness and the neighborhood wrath. She spoke softly to the little girl.

"What a nice father you have! I like him very much. And didn't you have a fine visit! Even Lilac had fun."

Gradually, the strain began to leave the child's face. Cherry talked on, softly, persistently.

After a while Mrs. Eldredge rose wearily. "Come, dear, time for sleep now."

After they had tucked Muriel into one of the high beds, Mrs. Eldredge led Cherry back to the deserted living room. They resumed their places before the fire.

"Well, Miss Ames, you have seen for yourself. The whole village knows and suspects. Your friend, Captain Wade, is probably hearing about it this very minute at the inn. And Mr. Heath, I fear, is going to add fuel to the fire."

Cherry studied the old, finely drawn face in the flickering firelight.

"One neighbor has complained about Mark to Scotland Yard!"

Cherry's black eyes widened. To report a man to Intelligence at Scotland Yard—the equivalent of the American FBI—was extremely serious. "What was done?"

"Nothing has happened to Mark so far. It probably is simply a question of time. Perhaps—possibly—Scotland Yard is still collecting evidence against him. The neighbors are furious about the delay. Muriel and I are—not precisely ostracized but—oh, the poor child!"

A little shiver went down Cherry's back.

Long after good-byes were said that night—and days after seeing Mark Grainger—one word kept tolling in Cherry's mind: "Spy. Spy. Spy." And just as persistently, some faith in Cherry replied:

"No!"

CHAPTER V

First Mission

CHERRY WAS TAKING A SHOWER ONE EARLY DECEMBER morning, before breakfast, when a whistle blew in the barracks shower room. Most of the Flight Three nurses ducked out of the stalls, dripping and in towels. Summoning them was Captain Betty Ryan already dressed in her uniform.

"Flight Three, you're alerted! Calls are coming from holding stations in the combat areas. Urgent! Don't stop for breakfast—get right down there on the line!"

Cherry and her fellow nurses ran back to their room, scrambled into their flight clothes—not the trim blue gabardine, but into tough, wind-resistant coveralls and heavy boots—and then ran to the landing field for all they were worth.

It was still dark on the airfield, windy and cold. Six C-47's were lined up, their engines humming. Cherry found Captain Cooper waiting for her.

"Get in, get in," he said urgently. "I've already cleared with base operations. Your sergeant is up there. We're going up to advance battle positions. Good luck!"

Wade boosted her up to the open bays. Bunce gave her a hand up, and she and Bunce slammed the heavy double doors. Cherry and Bunce sat down and strapped in, as their plane and the five alongside, quivered, roared, strained.

Cherry shouted above the racket, "This is our first test in a combat zone!"

"This is the real thing!" Bunce yelled back as they shook hands on it.

Now they heard the C-47 ahead of them taxi down the huge air strip and take off. It was Gwen's plane. Twenty seconds later their own aircraft started to rock, then skim over the ground. Cherry and Bunce held their breaths. They felt their plane tug—lift—lift again—again—

In a few more seconds, all the planes were up, roaring over the base. The noise was terrific. Cherry could see the other mighty brown ships in the foggy sky, flying with them in precise military formation. "Some beautiful flying!" she cried. Bunce was so thrilled he could only nod.

FIRST MISSION

"Did you get water? Sulfa? Blankets?" Cherry yelled.

"Yes, everything!" her technician yelled back.

She went back to the medical kit to lay out tourniquets, ointment for burns, and hypodermics. Bunce was pulling the webbing straps down into place. Cherry had a look at their cargo: medical supplies, mostly blood plasma. Not much for their huge transport to carry, but apparently the call came so suddenly, there was no time to load cargo.

Wade sent his copilot back into the cabin.

"Captain's compliments, Nurse!" Lieutenant Mason said. "Wants me to tell you our base notified the holding station when we took off. They'll be all ready and waiting for us. Captain says load the wounded as fast as possible—we may be under fire."

"Yes, sir! Are all six planes going to the same holding station?"

"No. We'll separate. Several holding stations, scattered all over the battle area! Excited?"

Cherry and Bunce grinned. Cherry admitted, "This is kind of different from our forty-five minute jaunt up to Prestwick. What's the flying time this trip?"

Bill Mason looked at his wrist watch. "Our base is an hour out of London. Twenty minutes to cross the English Channel. Half an hour to an hour more across enemy-held territory."

"Whew!" Bunce whistled. "Where're we going, sir?"

"Only Captain Cooper knows, Sergeant, and he's not saying. Well, kids, you have a couple of hours to get ready."

"We'll need it," Cherry said fervently. "Thanks a lot."

Lieutenant Mason saluted Cherry, nodded to Bunce, and started to go. He turned around awkwardly to say over the noise:

"Listen, kids. Take it from an old-time combat flier. Don't get too romantic about this mission. It's just a job to do—a job of muddy, hard work." Then he went up forward and disappeared behind the cockpit door.

Cherry and Bunce looked soberly at each other, then set to work. They made their preparations well—checked oxygen masks, got the sterilizer in the corner working, laid out coffee in the galley kit, put tubing on the blood plasma bottles. Cherry was too busy preparing for her soldier patients to be frightened, or to think at all. She saw the south of England floating by below, fields and towns turning from gray to their natural colors as the first rosy light of dawn crept over them. Then they were high over London, the Thames a silver thread below, the antique towers and domes and the myriad roofs turned to gold in the sun. But to Cherry, busy with her preparations, these were only brief, disconnected pictures. Until she happened to look down and see dark, churning water, she hardly realized they were well over the Channel. They must be within an hour of their destination. Time to clear with the pilot. Cherry made her way up forward.

"Captain—"

Wade did not turn. "Yes?" He was watching his course, as Ann's plane' veered out of formation to the east. They were all flying east now, east and slightly to the south.

"Captain," Cherry said loudly over the engine noise, "would you call the holding station and notify them we are a C-47 ready for eighteen litter cases."

"Right." Wade spoke into his interphone. "Dick? E.T.A. [Estimated Time of Arrival] Now 08 hours."

Cherry went back to the cabin.

"We're over enemy-held territory now," Bunce reminded her. "I sure wish we had a Red Cross painted on our plane."

Cherry saw the last two huge transports of their squadron veer off. They were flying alone now.

But not for long. She heard a different timbre, a different beat of engine roar, and looked out. Four small planes climbed up beside them, two on either side. They bristled with guns but—thank heavens!—on their side was painted the white star of American combat forces.

Wade's voice came through the interphone. "Don't be frightened, you two babies back there! Those are our own fighters—P-47's. They're escorting us up to the front."

Bunce mopped his brow. "That means we're within six miles of the holding station. Gosh, Miss Cherry—"

"Steady, Bunce." Cherry herself did not feel any too steady. She felt better, though, when she looked up and saw the four small, sturdy fighter planes flying above them.

Almost immediately they felt Wade circle and feel for a landing. Looking down, they saw a little hut or tent, and tiny figures running along a crude air strip.

"Here we are!" the pilot cried over the interphone. "We're going down! Cross your fingers."

Wade started down, circling, spiraling. Bunce muttered that this was a very tricky field on which to make a landing. The strip was a mile long but narrow and extremely crude. A figure below was motioning with a signal flag. Wade lifted the heavy aircraft, tried again. Down, down, down it went. The wheels touched the ground, the C-47 bounced—and had Cherry and Bunce not been strapped in, they would have been violently thrown. The plane skidded to a stop.

"All out!" Cherry cried. She and Bunce ran to open the doors.

The haggard face of an Army doctor peered in. Behind him, men on the field came running to the ambulance plane, crowding around.

"Hello, anybody home?" called the doctor in stained khaki. "I'm Major Wright."

"Lieutenant Ames, sir! Sergeant Smith."

"I certainly am glad to see you! You'll have to work fast."

Cherry and Bunce reached for outlifted hands and jumped to the ground. She heard one man exclaim, "A woman!"

"No nurses here, Major?"

"No, Lieutenant. Wish there were. We could use a few. But this is a holding station."

Cherry knew then that they were close to the front, as nurses stayed at least four miles back of the fighting. There was a sudden burst of artillery fire right in back of them, then more and more pounding away. They were not just close to the fighting front, Cherry thought, they were virtually in the middle of the battlefield! There was an urgent ring in the Major's voice. "We don't dare keep the wounded lying in a holding station more than half an hour. This place can be strafed any minute."

A captain came running up, with Wade behind him. He was the Evacuation Officer, who found the sites for the holding stations. Then the troops set down some kind of air strip.

"This working out all right with you, Lieutenant?" the Captain asked.

"Fine, fine," Cherry said and hurried after the Major. He led her into a tent, fixed up like a rough field hospital, for temporary care. Here, on litters on the ground, lay the pitiful men she had come for.

The Major briefly pointed out each casualty to Cherry and her technician. A stomach wound—a head wound—a back injury—some men were more seriously wounded. Among the eighteen wounded men they would take, only six absolutely helpless cases could go—no nurse could handle more.

"Sergeant, round up the loaders and you get back in the plane," Cherry directed.

The Major interrupted. "Wait, son. We have only two corpsmen who know how to load. Our other corpsmen are wounded—one killed. We'll have to use any ablebodied soldier who's around. We have an improvised ramp."

"You can count on me and my two crewmen to load," said Wade, right behind them. Cherry had not seen the pilot follow them. His face was pale and drawn.

"All right, Captain," Cherry said. "Start with this boy. Easy does it, soldier." She knelt beside a dirty-faced lad whose teeth were clenched in pain. His tag read internal injuries. "We're taking you home," Cherry said quickly. "You're going to be all right."

When he opened glazed eyes, and saw a nurse, he tried to smile.

Dick, Bill, Wade, and a corpsman from the holding station gently but quickly picked up his litter and carried him up the ramp. Cherry said to Bunce in a low voice, "Put him up forward and give him a shot of morphine. And hurry!"

The haggard doctor led Cherry among the litters, deciding which ones should go. One man, covered with mud and blood, fingered the edge of Cherry's trouser leg. He whispered, "Clean...."

"Compound fracture of the tibia, will have to operate," the Army doctor was classifying them. "This one lost a lot of blood. Incipient peritonitis, here."

But to Cherry they were not abstract cases. "They're just tired, dirty kids who've been shot up," she thought.

Bunce reported back to her. She drew him aside and told him what special medicines to get from the holding station for the trip.

There were too many wounded for them all to go on this trip. And still, over the rim of a little hill, from the sound of firing, came more ambulances loaded with wounded. The strings of ambulances jolted and bumped through the mud. Cherry thought of what even so small a thing as a rifle bullet can do to the human body, and was grateful for planes instead of those slow, jolting ambulances.

Cherry, with one eye on her watch, supervised the loading and placing of the litter cases, and hopped in the plane for a moment herself. The men were suffering but calm. They asked for nothing but water. Each time Cherry gave a man a drink, he smiled or tried to, and could not thank her enough. Cherry left the plane again—as the sixteenth litter was being carried up.

"I want you to take these two walking wounded," the doctor called to her.

Cherry turned. She saw one of the bravest and most pathetic sights she had yet seen in war. Limping, stumbling, leaning against each other, came two dazed boys, one with his arm flung about the other's neck. Their heads drooped under their heavy metal helmets, their breeches were split to the knee and bandages showed through. One boy all but fainted in Bunce's arms. The other boy protested:

"I only got a scratch! I don't want to go to the hospital! Let me go back to my outfit! I'm not quittin'! I have to get back to my outfit!"

Cherry saw that the back of his leather jacket was blood-soaked. They lifted him in, still protesting.

The casualties were all in now. Wade had gone up forward. The copilot already had the propellers spinning. The Army doctor hopped aboard to give last-minute instructions to Cherry.

"That internal injuries case." He rubbed his unshaven jaw. "I wish I could come along to look after him."

"Can't you, sir?"

The doctor looked back at Cherry from hollow eyes.

"I'm the only doctor here ... I'll notify England now that you're on your way. Well, good luck!"

Bunce slammed the doors shut. He had the patients all strapped in.

Wade strode in hurriedly but with a big smile on his face.

"Men, I'm your pilot. Name's Wade Cooper. I'll have you in England, in a real hospital, in a jiffy." His voice trembled. "Just take yourselves a good nap. Nurse Ames here, and the sergeant, will be looking out for you every minute."

Cherry took another precious moment to reassure the men. Their stricken faces showed they were listening. "Fellows, even if you've never been up before, don't worry. Captain Cooper is a crackerjack pilot. He's been in combat and—"

"I flew in North Africa in the old days," Wade said.

"Yes, sir, North Africa and around the Mediterranean—"

Cherry whispered hastily, "Before, you said China and Russia."

"Explain later. Altitudes?" They moved aside to talk altitudes for a moment. "Just relax, boys. You've earned it!" Wade half ran up the aisle of litters. Cherry saw relief in some of the faces as he passed, and climbed through the cockpit door.

Cherry sat down in the tail and strapped in. The plane started to vibrate. She happened to look out the low window, and nearly leaped out of her seat.

There, on this restricted military airfield, stood Mark Grainger! He wore shabby civilian clothes, an old hat pulled furtively over his smudged face. But it was Mark

Grainger and no mistake! He was hovering around a plane which was evidently a special plane. What was Mark Grainger—and obviously in disguise, too—doing here? All Cherry's suspicions were aroused. What if he were a spy ... Cherry's hands turned cold. She ought to warn someone—She could still stop the take-off—

But they were taxiing now. Too late.

Cherry sat back in the bucket seat feeling sick. Then she tore herself out of her strappings and threw herself flat beside the low window. Maybe she could get another glimpse—maybe when their ship circled and rose—Yes! There he was! She looked down to see Mark Grainger, a diminishing figure now, slipping away from the plane. Only now he carried a big shapeless bundle!

"Miss Cherry," Bunce asked anxiously, "are you sick?"

Cherry turned, and tried to pull herself together. These wounded men needed attention—Wade could not turn back now. Maybe Dick could radio a message. But what? No, it was too late.

"Miss Cherry! Miss Cherry!" Bunce put firm hands on her shoulders. "Here, drink this."

Automatically she swallowed an airsickness capsule in a little water. Sheer will, not the capsule, cleared her head. Her intense fright receded into calm. Seeing Mark Grainger here had been a shock. Well, she must put it out of her mind now. Her patients came first. She would ask Wade about that special-looking plane when they got home. Cherry went to her patients.

Their great aircraft had gained height and leveled off low, around six thousand feet. That was not a safe height but she was afraid some of the wounded could not stand higher altitudes. Four fighter planes rode at their sides. Some of the prone men were smiling with delight. "Going back," one whispered. They were going back to safety, to recovery, to life.

Now Cherry's real work began. She kept constant watch for oxygen need, as she moved from tier to tier. These soldiers were so grateful for the least little thing she did for them. They even thanked her for the clean, comfortable blankets. Not one complained.

Cherry gave blood plasma to the weakest—morphine to relieve one man's excruciating pain—told a depressed boy, "We'll fish that shell out of you and make it into a medal." She was shaken at the awful human waste of war. She could not give definitive care: she could only keep these men from getting worse, give a little comfort, until she got them to a hospital and surgeons. These wounded were extra-special patients.

"Nurse, my leg aches. The splint presses."

"Please, Nurse—water—"

"Why is it so dark?"

The wounded followed Cherry around with weary eyes. One shocked boy stared into space. Cherry gave him a sedative to induce sleep.

"Nurse, you really here? I ain't dreamin'?"

"Mm, your perfume. Smells like the stuff my girl uses."

A boy with a gunshot wound in his abdomen became delirious. In his thoughts he was still at the battlefield. Cherry gave him a hypodermic, quieted him, kept her cool hand on his forehead. He cried out, "Mother! Mother! I knew you'd come!" Cherry held him in her arms, as his mother would have done, until his wrenching pain gave way to drugged sleep.

She cleaned a bad chest wound, bound up a smashed hand, gave oxygen to a fainting man with a head injury. One boy clutched at her ankle as she passed. She knelt beside his bottom tier.

"How're you doing, soldier?"

He started to cry.

"Please don't. You'll be all right. I'll bring you some hot coffee." She smiled and patted his shoulder. "Sound good to you?"

"Yes." He dragged his hand across his tear-wet face. "Coffee. Thank you."

Cherry and Bunce were so busy that they hardly noticed their fighter escort was gone now and the riding was bumpy. The copilot came back with a message.

"We're going to have to climb, Nurse."

"But we can't climb! My men can't stand it—I don't want to give them oxygen!"

"Have to go up. Don't ask me why."

They climbed, and Cherry sent Bunce to put the oxygen masks on the patients. It was getting chilly and it was hard to breathe. Cherry was uneasy. She ran up to see the pilot, getting out her own mask.

"What's the matter?" she cried.

"Radio advises enemy planes spotted. Go back and keep those men calm."

Up and up they went. The medicine chest was torn out of its brace. Wade was trying to dodge the enemy planes by climbing, by straining the engines to utmost speed. Some of the wounded began to ask questions.

Cherry struggled to hold a plasma bottle steady and said in a loud, confident voice, "It's nothing, fellows, nothing! We just make better time a little higher up. All right, Sergeant, hand me the needle. Steady now, boy, this'll make you stronger—*No*, it's nothing to worry about! I promise!"

The men were scared. Cherry was scared, too, but she dared not let them see it. Eighteen helpless men looked to her for courage. She was actress now—actress, leader, mother—as well as nurse.

"Feels funny, this place where my leg used to be. My ex-leg."

"The doctors will fix you up. You—" the plane lurched but Cherry steadied herself and went on talking, "—you'll be able to walk again, as you always did. Bunce, strap this corporal down good and comfortable."

She ran to the tail and looked out. They were over the Channel. Good! Maybe they were leaving the German planes behind. Maybe they'd meet no Messerschmitts over the Channel. Wade must have outraced them—pulled this precious cargo through!

Then they were dropping. Through the clouds, Cherry saw faintly the cliffs of England.

Another hour of intense work, of terrific strain, while Cherry drew on her every ounce of training and common sense and tact and physical strength. She was exhausted now, but she kept on doing her best for her planeful of wounded, until they were over the trees of their own neighborhood. They were going down, gently, down, and circling.

Wade put them down as if laying a baby in its cradle. Cherry and Bunce spoke encouragement to their patients, and opened the doors.

Ambulances were waiting, and the unloading teams were ready. Major Thorne, the Flight Surgeon, entered the plane immediately. Cherry stayed in the plane door watching the blinded boy, the man with a wound in his abdomen, and the patient with a chest wound, gently being lifted out. The men's faces were too exhausted to show much emotion. Some of them lifted their eyes to Cherry's as they passed, some murmured good-bye. She said warmly to all of them, "Good luck to you!"

FIRST MISSION

The men were unloaded quickly and rushed to the hospital. Cherry made her report to Major Thorne, while Wade reported to base operations, and came back for her.

Captain Betty Ryan appeared too, smiling. "Good for you, Lieutenant Ames! Are you all right? You show signs of flying fatigue. I don't like that, Cherry. I want you to take a twenty-four hour rest, starting now. It's for your own good, Cherry."

"I could use a rest," Cherry admitted wearily to Wade, as they walked across home field unloosening their heavy jackets.

"I could use some food," Wade said. "Come on, honey. Let's see what grub we can find in the Fliers' Club."

At the deserted club, the two of them sank down onto a sofa. A waitress brought them bowls of steaming, reviving soup. It was only two o'clock in the afternoon, but Cherry felt she had lived through a week, since she got out of the shower that morning.

After she and Wade had relaxed for a while, Cherry asked:

"Well, Captain? Are you more reconciled to your job now?"

He curled his hand over hers. "Quite a job, isn't it? But, Cherry, you were magnificent." He lifted her hand and kissed it.

"Now, don't get romantic."

"Why not?" he asked. "Is there someone else?"

"In a way. There was—there used to be." She was thinking guiltily of Lex.

"There still is?"

"I don't know," Cherry replied honestly. "I haven't seen him for a year. There was never anything definite between us. But—well, you know."

Wade declared cheerfully, "If that's all, if it's just loyalty to a dead issue, I refuse to be scared out. Waitress! What can you feed us?"

After they had started in on substantial sandwiches, Cherry put her original question again.

Wade grinned and slowly shook his head. "We-ell—I want to do the best I can for those beat-up boys. But some day, after I've done my penance in this branch, I hope they'll put me back in combat flying. This is too tame."

Cherry smiled. "So you still feel like a nursemaid!"

"Let's talk about something else, huh?"

"Yes, there is something I want to talk over with you," Cherry said soberly. She waited until Wade ordered two Coca-Colas and poured them.

She told him, without reserve now, all she knew of the story of Mark Grainger. Wade listened closely. Then Cherry told him she had seen Mark Grainger that morning on the restricted military airfield.

"He was hanging around a special sort of plane."

"Yes, Cherry. I know the plane you mean."

"What's that plane used for?"

Captain Cooper hesitated. "I have no right to tell you."

"And yet, Wade, I have to know. If this man should be a spy—"

Wade took a long sip of his Coke, considering. "All right. But keep it quiet. The plane he was loitering around is for carrying paratroops—infantry who drop from that plane by parachute, into enemy country or enemy-occupied countries. You see, they go in in a surprise attack."

"And Mark Grainger might be forestalling the surprise? And then when the paratroopers hit the silk, there might be enemy troops waiting for them.... What was in his bundle, do you suppose?"

"No telling. Dynamite, possibly. Paratroops carry that."

Cherry tiredly pushed her black curls off her forehead. "It sounds bad. But I just can't believe it of Muriel's father."

Wade pulled her head down on his shoulder. "Now quit worrying. You're so tired, your imagination is running wild. You, little lady, shouldn't be thinking of anything but sleep right now, and leave prowling spies for manhandling by Intelligence." He grinned at her. "Besides, he probably isn't a spy at all!"

Cherry said gratefully, "Good old common-sense Cooper." She thought that if this were Lex instead of Wade—Lex with his seriousness and rather heavy intensity—the air would not be cleared so quickly and happily.

"Could we do some sleuthing?" she asked.

"And where are we to get the time or freedom to go chasing spies all over the country? No, ma'am. The only place you're going now is off to your little bunk."

Five minutes later, Cherry was snuggling down into her pillow and blankets. Wade was right. She was very tired, very, very tired. Never in her whole life could she remember having been as tired as this. The question of Mark Grainger would have to wait.

CHAPTER VI

A Medal for Johnny

THE NEXT TIME CHERRY FLEW TO THE SAME HOLDING station, Mark Grainger was nowhere in sight. No special plane for paratroopers was parked on that air strip, either. Cherry saw that the instant her plane landed.

She followed Major Wright into the rough tent, wondering whether she should say something about the furtive visitor she had seen the other day. But the Army doctor was preoccupied in classifying the men who lay on litters.

Besides, the guns sounded sickeningly close today, and there was no time to linger. Their casualties might be strafed as they were being lifted into the hospital plane! She urged the volunteer loaders to lift the litters aboard as fast as possible.

In less than ten minutes, they were loaded. The doctor had given Cherry last-minute instructions about the eighteen litter cases aboard, and Bunce was slamming the plane doors shut. Cherry strapped in and waited anxiously for the take-off. She had some bad cases aboard today.

Wade took the plane up swiftly. Their four fighter escorts were flying steadily just above them. Cherry did not wait until they had leveled off to get to her strange ward.

"Nurse!"

She stood on tiptoe to peer at a sergeant lying on a top tier. He was an older man, badly shot up.

"Water, Sergeant?"

"No—never mind me! Is that boy all right? He's in my company. I saw him get it this morning. He took it deliberately—saved at least six of us."

"I'll find him. Don't worry."

Cherry followed the sergeant's anxious gaze and went to the next tier. There, in a middle stretcher, with one man lying below him on the plane floor, and two men slung above him, lay a stocky, very young soldier. Cherry noticed that although these other tired, dirty men had dark shadows of beard on their jaws, this boy was clean-shaven. His eyes were closed.

"Hello," Cherry said softly. "How're you making out, soldier?"

He opened his eyes and stared at her. Perhaps he was too dazed to speak. Cherry put her hand on his

A MEDAL FOR JOHNNY

smooth cheek. Sometimes just the reassuring touch of the nurse's hand was enough to calm a frightened patient. But Cherry had a surprise coming.

"I'm perfectly jake. Go away!"

Cherry took his pulse and respiration. "You could be better. I'm going to give you a hot drink, and change those bandages."

"Go away, will you? Let me alone!"

Cherry glanced up in some confusion at the sergeant, who was looking down on this scene. For some reason, the older man was grinning. Something was up. What was it?

Cherry went ahead with the dressings while the young soldier grumbled. He had a bad leg, and his right arm and hand lay useless on the stretcher. Cherry gave him a stimulant, too, carefully regulating the dose of medicine to their altitude. She was trying to give this boy, as she did with each patient, as much individual care as possible.

"*Now* will you go away?" he scolded.

Cherry grinned at this youth. Freckles spattered over a turned-up nose, clear brown eyes and a broken tooth in front made him look very young indeed.

"You look about fourteen years old," Cherry teased, as she finished the treatment. "Why are you so eager to get rid of me?"

The man on the tier above said weakly, "Shall we tell her, Sergeant? She's guessed it, anyway."

"Want to tell me?" Cherry asked the scowling boy. She realized now that a full half of the men lying in the swaying plane were watching, amused but concerned too.

Suddenly the truth hit her. The others were all unshaven—this boy was smooth-faced—he had squirmed when she said he looked only fourteen years old—

"Why," she exclaimed, "you *are* only fourteen."

"Fourteen and a half!" he said indignantly. "And don't you dare tell on me!"

Laughter spread weakly from tier to tier. Cherry worked from man to man. Each one begged her not to report Johnny. She was glad they had something to talk about, to distract them from their pain. Even a fractured knee, a smashed pelvis, a pleurisy-tuberculosis case, and a back full of shrapnel fragments, seemed less terrible on this trip. The soldiers were absorbed in making their special pleas for Johnny.

"He had our whole company fooled. You know we shave every day if it's at all possible. Didn't suspect until these last three days. We were in those foxholes for three days and nights without moving. Couldn't shave."

"Nurse, be a good sport about Johnny, won't you? He's one of the best GI's in our outfit. He took it on the chin for our platoon this morning."

"Don't tell on the kid! It'd break his heart to be mustered out of the Army and sent home to school!"

A MEDAL FOR JOHNNY

Finally Cherry burst out laughing. She made this announcement, not only to Johnny, but to all of them:

"Fellows, I ought to report Johnny but I won't. Just the same, someone is sure to find out when you're all in the hospital. You see, the corpsmen will come around with shaving things—and believe me, those doctors and nurses have sharp eyes."

Johnny called stubbornly, "I won't let 'em catch me. I'm *not* going home!"

Cherry shook her head doubtfully but she had to laugh again. She was impressed, too, at the spunk of this boy. He must have run away from home and fibbed his way into the Army. His parents probably were worried to distraction about this youthful adventurer.

The flight back to the base hospital went off almost cheerfully, because Johnny was aboard.

As the men were being unloaded, Cherry whispered to the fourteen-(and-a-half)-year-old boy, "I'll come to the hospital to see you!"

He scowled up from his litter. "Don't you write my ma!"

"No. Promise."

Cherry was too busy for the next few days, and also too tired, to get over to the hospital to see the underage soldier. She was a little puzzled over her continuing fatigue. The other flight nurses admitted they too found this work a terrific strain. But they perked up after a long sleep, and somehow, Cherry did not. However, she pushed herself and kept going—more flights into combat areas, helping out on wards, preparing for the next flight.

There was not a moment to see Muriel or Mrs. Eldredge now. Cherry debated as to whether or not she should tell Mrs. Eldredge that she had actually seen Mark Grainger on a forbidden military airfield, in the heart of the combat area. It certainly made things look bad for him. What had he been doing there? If he were a spy—

A spy could make real trouble in that spot. A spy could tip off the enemy that this was where the unprotected wounded lay. A spy could learn for the enemy the comings and goings of paratroop planes, for this air strip apparently was used for more purposes than evacuating the wounded. A spy could walk only two or three miles from the holding station and be at a headquarters tent, where written orders and marked maps for the battles to come were kept. A spy in this critical spot—with, perhaps, a load of dynamite—Cherry's head ached at the endless and terrible possibilities.

If Mark Grainger were a spy, could the sentries actually have been so lax as to let him through? Yet an occasional slip-up was almost bound to occur. Mark could have slipped in, unnoticed, or he could even have come in quite legally, by pretending to be a neighboring farmer with food to sell to the Army. There were a dozen ways for a clever, fearless man to get in.

A MEDAL FOR JOHNNY

How did he get across the Channel? That was another, and thorny, question. Certainly not on that carefully restricted plane he was hanging around.

Should she tell Mrs. Eldredge? It was a heavy question.

"I'd better not do or say anything until I'm sure," Cherry thought. "It would only worry Mrs. Eldredge unnecessarily." She recalled her talk with Wade. "After all, we don't have anything very definite to base any charges on. It looks suspicious, but I don't *know*."

Once more, the picture of Mark Grainger playing with his little daughter, in that peaceful sitting room, returned to Cherry. There popped into her head the reproachful words—"O ye of little faith!"

She did have faith in Mark Grainger, suspicions notwithstanding. Muriel's faith in her father was the basis for it. Children were not easily deceived, Cherry thought; children had a basic, unspoiled honesty which sensed dishonesty in others, particularly in those they loved. Perhaps Muriel's innocent trust in her father was the true barometer of Mark Grainger's worth.

So when Cherry finally had a little free time, the following week, she used it not to pursue her suspicions, but to visit fourteen-(and-a-half)-year-old Johnny.

At the hospital, Cherry applied for entrance and cleared with the Information authorities, like any other visitor. Then she went upstairs to a ward she had never seen before. She was curious to see how some of those men, who were transported on her plane the other day, were getting along.

The minute Cherry entered the ward, she was heartened. The long white room was badly overcrowded—jammed with extra rows of beds—but these young men were getting well! It was absolutely amazing how quickly they snapped back to health and high spirits. A radio was playing swing music. Some of the fellows were already strolling around the ward visiting. Those still in the beds were joking with the Red Cross ladies as they played checkers or learned to knit woolen socks. It was hard to recognize the beat-up soldiers out of the foxholes in these clean, cheerful lads. "Our young men have the stamina and resilience of steel wire!" Cherry thought proudly. "And what unquenchable spirit!"

They were talking, she discovered, about their chances of being flown home to America—talking eagerly. Planes did a lot for morale!

Cherry located Johnny hunched up in bed. He was not a bit glad to see her. In fact, he pulled the covers over his face. Cherry pulled them down again. A pair of fiery boyish eyes snapped at her.

"I s' pose you've come to report me!"

Cherry laughed. "Nothing of the sort. But haven't they caught you yet?"

Johnny looked around guardedly. "They're beginning to suspect," he whispered. "But they still don't know."

A MEDAL FOR JOHNNY

He gave her an impish grin. Out of uniform, he certainly did look like the schoolboy he was.

Cherry took a look at his chart, hanging on his bed. It said that Johnny was a long way from recovery. Although he did not know it, Johnny was slated to return to a hospital in the United States for long-term convalescent care. Somewhere along the way, he would surely be discovered and retired from the Army—though of course the Army would keep him in a hospital until he was thoroughly well again. Johnny was not going to like what lay ahead.

Cherry looked into his scowling, freckled face, and considered. Better for him to face the inevitable with the right attitude. She was the only Army Medical Corps person who knew of his plight. She had a responsibility here. She must try to make Johnny face the facts with a more grown-up attitude.

"Quite a flight we had the other day," she started. "How would you like to fly home?"

"Not goin' home!"

"But suppose the Army ordered you back home, for medical treatment?"

"Too risky, sittin' around a hospital. I'm goin' to get out of this hospital, or any hospital, *quick*—'fore anybody catches me."

Cherry shrugged. She apparently was not going to get very far on her first try. "Bet you a stick of chewing gum that I can beat you at checkers," she dared him.

Johnny reluctantly grinned. "You're not so bad. Okay, it's a bet."

She let him win. They parted good friends, but with Johnny as stubborn as ever.

The next afternoon, over another furious game of checkers, Cherry tried another tack.

"I spent the whole morning writing letters," she mentioned casually. "Do you write home often to your folks?"

"Naw. Never write at all."

"Tough guy, aren't you?"

Johnny suddenly looked his age. He bluffed, "Sure, I'm tough. How could I write my folks? If my ma knew where I was, she'd get me home faster'n—well, too fast. Naw. I just don't write at all."

Cherry jumped his king with her single. He was exasperated but impressed. Johnny did not enjoy losing. She seized his little discomfiture to make her next words sink in.

"Your mother must be awfully worried about you."

"Aw, she knows I can take care of myself."

Cherry did not press the point but chatted instead of other things. She exerted herself to win that game, and the next. Her winning weakened Johnny's aggressiveness a little, made him vulnerable to Cherry's next words. She aimed them carefully.

"I'm glad I'm not your mother. I guess she's half out of her mind with worry about you."

A MEDAL FOR JOHNNY

This time Johnny's round eyes showed concern. "Honestly? I never thought about that. I wouldn't want to—to make her feel bad, or nuthin'. Ma's swell."

Cherry sharply changed her tactics. "You know, Johnny," she said again, casually, "I admire you a lot. As a soldier, you're really a grown man."

"Thanks, Lieutenant."

"But you ought to grow up."

"Grow up!" Johnny sat up, indignant and excited. "Didn't you just say I'm a good soldier?"

"Ssh! I mean, grow up in the sense that you face reality."

"Foxholes are real enough!"

"And another reality is that a fourteen-year-old boy is illegally in the Army. If you were really a good soldier, you wouldn't want to break the regulations."

"Yeah." Johnny lay back on his pillow, thoughtful.

"I'll come around tomorrow," Cherry said, rising from her chair. "If you feel like writing letters tomorrow, I'll be glad to write 'em for you."

"So long," said Johnny shortly. Cherry left him with plenty to think about.

On her third visit, there was no checker game. Just talk—and a letter to Johnny's mother. Cherry sat at the boy's bedside with paper and pen.

"What'll I say?" he demanded. "You got me into this! Now tell me what to say."

"Well, tell her you're in the Army. In a hospital, but not too badly hurt," Cherry suggested.

"In a hospital! You think I want to *worry* Ma?"

Cherry smothered a laugh. "Well, how about this? You're undoubtedly going to get some sort of recognition for saving those men in your company—a Purple Heart, at least. Your mother would be proud to know that."

"I should say not! She'd think I was beat-up for sure. Sure, it was machine-gun bullets, and I bled a little, but I'm not really hurt. And what can you do with a medal anyway?"

"Well, tell her you'll probably be seeing her soon."

Johnny's freckled face grew mournful. "They're really going to send me back?"

"It looks like it."

"And then I'll have to go back to school. 'Discharged for bein' too young!' What a reason! Me, a fightin' man, saying, 'Yes, ma'am' to the teacher!"

Cherry nearly laughed at this schoolboy patriot, but she sympathized with him. While Johnny muttered that he was "strictly GI" and "they can't do this to me," Cherry wrote a very creditable letter to his mother. Johnny finally approved it and Cherry tucked it in her pocket to mail.

Well, she had won half her point. The other half—Johnny's reconciliation to being mustered out—was still to be managed, somehow.

A MEDAL FOR JOHNNY

Cherry did not manage it. A General did.

The Commanding General came into the ward an afternoon later. Cherry happened to be at the bedside of the intractable Johnny. An electric thrill went through the ward. The convalescing soldiers, even those in bed, tried to come to attention.

"At ease!" the General said. He was smiling. He was dressed in the same simple windbreaker and trousers. and trench cap as infantrymen wear, except for the stars on his shoulder. He said, "I'm glad to see you're all improving. "I've been reading reports about you men. Fine reports."

He beckoned to the two aides behind him who were carrying typed papers and a small box.

The General stepped over to the first bed and bent down to greet the sergeant who had been on Cherry's top tier. "Sergeant Jerry Kowolwicz, for bravery in action," he read from his report. "Sergeant, the Army wants to award you this decoration. Fine work, sir! Hope you'll be up and out of here soon." They shook hands.

"Thank you, General," said the sergeant as the whole ward applauded.

From bed to bed went the General. Cherry tingled with excitement as he told in ringing tones what these Americans had done. She moved back into the aisle as she saw that the General was coming to Johnny's bed!

Johnny, sitting up, was pale with excitement. Each freckle stood out plainly and his eyes were round as a puppy's. The General marched up to his bedside and smiled at the boy.

"Well, Private Kane, you're a little younger than I expected—from such a record!" He read for the whole ward to hear, "Private John Kane, for extraordinary courage under fire and selfless devotion to his comrades!" The ward broke into applause for Johnny, even before the General bent to pin a medal on Johnny's pajama top.

"Wait just a moment, sir?" Johnny remonstrated respectfully.

He hopped out of bed on his one good leg, and stood at attention.

"—award you the very high decoration—the Distinguished Service Cross for heroism!"

The applause was deafening. The General applauded too. Cherry clapped her hands till they burned. When it had quieted down a bit, the General said,

"Tell me, son. How old are you?"

There was silence. You could have heard a pin drop. All the men were poker-faced. Cherry watched Johnny hard.

He gulped. "I'm fourteen and a half, sir," he admitted.

"Well, I'll be—!" The General shook the boy's hand and he himself helped Johnny back into bed. "You little rascal!"

Johnny held out until after the General had made all the awards, and left. Then he pulled the covers up over his face. Cherry went and peeked underneath. The boy was sobbing into his pillow.

She stroked his hair. He seized her hand and held on tight.

"I—I did the right thing, though!" he choked out.

"You certainly did and it took courage. I'm awfully proud of you! Your mother will be thrilled!"

He sniffed loudly. "Well, anyhow, I won't mind so much—goin' back to school—with a D. S. C. pinned on me! I'm satisfied to go now. You were right, at that, even if you are a girl. You—you win!"

The last Cherry ever saw of Johnny, he was smiling, and waving good-bye to her from his bed.

CHAPTER VII

Christmas Party

CHERRY'S CHRISTMAS STARTED AT SIX A.M. WHEN THE bugle notes of reveille echoed around the hills. She climbed out of bed eagerly. Today was not only Christmas but her birthday. Though her birthday was really December twenty-fourth, Cherry was celebrating it today. She looked out the barracks window hoping to see snow. A light powder of frost lay on the British earth and trees.

"Back home," she thought, "in the good old U.S.A., and especially in Hilton, Illinois, I'll bet the snow's knee-deep—trees groaning with the weight of it!"

It was going to be lonely, not being able to spend her Christmas-birthday at home, with her family. Perhaps there would be letters from home for her today. There should be. Cherry was a little disappointed that no Christmas packages had arrived as yet. Where were they?

The girls were waking up, lazing a little this holiday morning. Only Elsie and Agnes had flight orders today. They were disappointed, because all the flight nurses were giving a Christmas party for the children of the near-by villages. It was Bunce's idea, originally. Everybody was pitching in, though, to make the party a success.

"First, I absolutely must get my mail!" Cherry declared.

Gwen and Ann grinned at each other. "We have your mail, dear. We've had it hidden away for three days."

"You wretches!"

"Oh, we know you! We know you could never hold out till your birthday to open your presents!"

"Give them to me right away!" Cherry implored.

Gwen said solicitously, "Not on an empty stomach?"

Cherry shrieked. "Yes, before breakfast! Come on now—hand them over!"

Flight Three was enjoying the joke hugely. Ann and Gwen dug Cherry's packages out of their foot lockers. The whole flight looked on appreciatively as Cherry unwrapped her birthday-Christmas gifts. There was food from Cherry's mother—which by unspoken Army agreement was community property—a tiny camera and some precious rolls of film from Cherry's father.

Midge sent impractical, lace-edged, crepe underthings, but Cherry was glad to see "something civilized" again. Dr. Joe sent a book; he always sent that. For the first time in Cherry's life, there was no present from her twin brother, Charlie, though she had sent him one, months before. She was disappointed but realized the Army Air Forces must be sending Charlie to places where there were no knickknacks to buy. There was no present from Lex, either, though Cherry really did not expect one.

"A very respectable haul," Gwen declared loyally. "My vote goes for the pretties Midge sent."

"There isn't much you can give someone in service," Ann said. "However, Gwen and I did find you these."

"These" were a beautifully tooled leather writing case, and a quaint old silver powder box. Cherry was really pleased with these typically English souvenirs.

She had presents for her two old friends, too. "Don't know how you'll ever get these home, but here they are." It was Cherry's turn to dig puppy-fashion in her foot locker. She handed Ann a blue Wedgwood teapot, "to match your eyes, Annie." And for Gwen she had a pair of tawny tortoise-shell combs.

So everyone was completely happy.

"Mail for you, too, Cherry," Gwen confessed. She took a handful of letters from her seemingly bottomless foot locker.

The girls began to troop out to breakfast. "Coming, Cherry?"

"What, with all these letters to feast on!"

"I'll bring you some coffee," Ann promised, patting Cherry's black curls. "Happy birthday!"

Cherry curled up on her bed, in the deserted barracks room. Six letters to read and enjoy—from her mother, her dad, Charlie, Dr. Joe, Midge Fortune, and finally Lex. Cherry stacked them in that order and eagerly started to read.

Mrs. Ames wrote a good, satisfying letter about home. It was full of little details about the house, the neighbors, and the antics of Midge who was staying with Mr. and Mrs. Ames while her father, Dr. Fortune, was in the Army Medical Corps. "I miss you, Cherry," her mother wrote. "Frankly, I worry about you. I would be just as well satisfied if the Army Nurse Corps would send you back to the United States."

"I wouldn't be satisfied, Mother," Cherry replied silently. "What an odd idea for you to think up! Never mind, I'll write you a long, newsy letter soon."

Her father was not much of a hand at letter writing, leaving that chore to Mrs. Ames. Nevertheless, when Cherry opened his V-mail, she burst into giggles. Reproduced on the tiny page was a tiny airplane and a girl—labeled C. A.—hanging onto the tail. Her father's drawing was so bad, and his idea of her job so strange, that Cherry sat and shook with laughter. "This bee-you-tee-ful picture from your loving Dad," he wrote.

Charlie had sent a V-mail also, two of them in fact. Cherry bent over his close typing.

"Congratulate me. I am," he wrote, "a hero by mistake. I was flying down a mountain pass here in—— and came to two passes that looked exactly alike. I mean they——. I was flying by map. Just when I was getting good and worried, I saw a field with a dozen—— so I went down in a surprise dive and set them afire. When I got back, it took my commander and me two hours of studying our maps to figure out what field I'd shot up so neatly. Seems I'd been two hundred miles north of where I had intended to be! No medals for this, either! It's a gyp."

Cherry grinned. She'd have to show Wade this letter, even if it started him wishing for combat flying again. Wade and Charlie certainly would understand each other. Cherry puzzled over the blanks in her twin's letter. It sounded as if Charlie were somewhere in the Orient, possibly Burma.

"I'd give a nickel, pal, to see you right now," Cherry thought. No doubt her brother felt the same way on this, their mutual birthday.

Dr. Joe's letter was all about his work, in general. Not a word about the Mark Grainger matter except at the very end. "Mrs. Eldredge has written me that you came to call on her. She said she finds you 'helpful.' I trust you will discover nothing serious, Cherry."

"I hope not!" Cherry thought. But at the moment Midge's fat, bursting envelope was clamoring to be read.

"Dearest Duck (that's an English expression), I think about you all the time up there in your *romantic* airplane. I'll bet all your patients fall in love with you." Cherry smiled but shook her curly head. Midge had a blissfully ignorant idea of those flights as joy rides. "You'd hardly know me. I've grown another inch and wear my hair a new way. Your mother said I couldn't use lipstick yet—chiefly because she says I smear on too much—and I guess she's right. School is still wearing me down. But I keep thinking, 'Oh, well, I'll be a nurse yet!' so I suffer willingly. I wrote to the U.S. Cadet Nurse Corps at that address you gave me—Box 88, New York—and Box 88 wrote me back a real nice letter. Maybe I'll win one of those nursing scholarships yet. Box 88, I love you! I am also slightly in love with two boys in my class, but I guess when you love two boys at once, you don't really love either one. So I will wait a while, because anyway I still have to pass Intermediate Algebra. Lots and lots of love, Midge."

"P.S. I sent you some simply lush undies. Hope you like them."

"P.P.S. Do you think it is possible to care for two boys at once? Midge."

Cherry put the letter down with a smile. Tomboy Midge—wanting to use lipstick and worrying about love!

Cherry turned to her own love department—the letter from Lex. Their romance seemed a long time ago to Cherry. But a letter from Lex was still saved to read at the last.

His first sentence puzzled her: "Dear Cherry, This is going to be a difficult letter to write. But I would rather you heard this news from me, not from anyone else. Yet I hardly know how to tell you."

Cherry read on, with a sinking feeling in the pit of her stomach.

"I asked you to marry me on several occasions, but you always put me off, saying you were not yet ready for marriage. Even when I finally persuaded you to accept the ring which was my grandmother's, you still did not feel you could regard it as an engagement ring. I did understand how you felt, Cherry, believe me.

"During this past year another girl has come into my life. We have fallen in love with each other and by the time this letter reaches you in England, we will be married."

Cherry slowly put the letter down. She could not see to read through the tears in her eyes. Lex married! She waited a moment, then read Lex's last few words.

"I don't flatter myself that this news will hurt you.

You never really cared for me, I know. It was a beautiful friendship, though, and I am grateful for it. Please keep the ring in pleasant memory of your old and devoted friend, Lex."

Cherry dropped the letter and frankly wept. She let the sobs tear at her, then suddenly thought:

"What am I really crying about? I never loved Lex—he's right. I never really wanted to marry him and spend the rest of my life with him."

She sat up very straight and rubbed her eyes hard. Just the same a terribly forsaken feeling pervaded her. The pang would not go away.

She scolded herself for feeling this way. Surely she did not begrudge Lex his happiness with another girl. And yet—and yet—the mingled sweetness and pain left her puzzled.

Ann opened the door, faithfully bringing Cherry some coffee. When she saw Cherry sitting there with an empty, faraway look in her eyes, she put her arm about her.

"Why, sweetie, what's wrong?"

Cherry shrugged. "Maybe just hurt vanity," she said accurately enough. "Lex—has married another girl."

"Well, that's nice," said Ann. "I know it hurts, but after all, dear, Lex wasn't for you."

"Lex wasn't for me," Cherry echoed. Ann was generally penetrating and understanding. This time, again, Ann was right. Cherry had never found Lex much fun, though she admired him. Yet the hauntingly sweet ache persisted.

"Drink your coffee," Ann urged gently.

The hot drink steadied her a bit. Cherry washed her face. But she still felt unhappy.

"I'll leave you alone," Ann said tactfully. "I came back to tell you something, but I guess this isn't the moment."

"No, do tell me, Ann."

"Well! Jack just wrote me—in our own private code—that he believes his outfit is coming to England. He says this time, at long last, we're going to be married. Even if he has to break all Army regulations to do it!" Ann's grave blue eyes were glowing.

"Oh, Annie, I'm so glad for you! You and Jack have waited so long."

Cherry was genuinely glad. Yet after Ann had left, Ann's happiness in love only made Cherry feel more desolate.

There was a tap on the window. Cherry went and opened it. Grinning in the frosty air was Wade Cooper.

"Merry Christmas! Don't you want your present?"

He impudently leaned through the window and kissed her.

"Oh, that's not the present," he said laughing. "Here!"

He gave her a billowing white silk scarf. He had had it made especially for her—from a parachute that had once saved his life.

"Why, Wade," Cherry breathed.

Suddenly life was wonderful again. That forsaken, desolate feeling amazingly evaporated. She leaned out the window and hugged her pilot, to the astonishment of Major Thorne and three corporals who were passing by.

It was not too difficult, after that, for Cherry to write Lex. She assured him she was honestly happy to hear of his happiness—"if you chose her, she must be nice"—thanked him for the ring which she would certainly treasure—and wound up with her very best good wishes to him and his bride. She pounded the stamp on the envelope, and with a light heart, went out to mail it, and to help get things ready for the Christmas party.

But she turned back. Good heavens! She had omitted sending a Christmas greeting to Mrs. Eldredge! She could still catch the mail corporal who was driving in to the villages. He would deliver it for her. Cherry raced back into the barracks and found a pretty card. She sat there biting the end of her pen. She wanted this to be a cheerful, hopeful message. Finally she wrote:

"Merry Christmas! I hope this finds you well and having a happy holiday, and *not* worrying! I feel more sure than ever there is really nothing to worry about. All my best wishes."

There! She hoped that might help. Now, off to Officers' Mess hall to get ready for the children's party.

Cherry saw that the long tables in the mess hall had been taken down. A circle of nurses were laughing their heads off. She wiggled her way into the circle. Major Thorne was rehearsing for his role as Santa Claus. Major Thorne was naturally jolly and plump—so plump the nurses did not need to stuff him with the pillow someone had brought.

"I'm well built for the role," he jested. He beamed benignly in the baggy red suit Flight One had made for him. Then he submitted to having a long white beard, fashioned from cotton and muslin strips, fitted to his several chins.

"Will it fall off if I sneeze?" he asked.

"*Don't* sneeze, sir!" he was warned.

Not needed here, Cherry wandered off to give a hand with the refreshments. Powdered milk and powdered eggs, with a dash of flavoring and nutmeg, was turning into a fine eggnog. "Skinny little Muriel and those other undernourished little kids can use plenty of that," Cherry thought. She offered to help, but was told to go inquire about the steak.

"Steak!" Cherry cried incredulously. "Where did you get steak in wartime Britain?"

These nurses, too, burst into laughter "See Private Jones in the kitchen," was all they would say. Mystified, Cherry went into the kitchen and inquired for Private Jones.

A sober youth in uniform advised her how the steak was obtained.

"I was doing guard duty last night. I heard someone moving around in the trees. I shouted 'Halt! Who goes there?' No answer. Just more footsteps and stuff. So I challenged again and waited for the password. This person in the bushes says: 'Moo! Moo!' Now you know yourself, ma'am, that 'Moo' wasn't the password. So I had to shoot him."

Cherry collapsed on a flour barrel and laughed till her sides ached.

"You'll probably get court-martialed for shooting somebody's cow," she finally managed to gasp out.

"That cow was trespassing on a military area," the boy said sternly. "Any self-respecting cow would have learned the password."

Well, that seemed to take care of refreshments. Cherry went to see if she could help with the decorations. The girls were just starting.

"Oh, sure," they said. "We need a good climber to fix up the tree."

So Cherry stood on a ladder and festooned the fir tree with strings of hard candy, in variegated colors. It looked festive and, besides, small guests always preferred decorations they could eventually pop into small mouths. Then Cherry sprinkled salts on the pine branches, carefully avoiding the candy. The tree emerged with a crystal-like sparkle.

Little Maggie was earnestly cutting out a Merry Christmas sign from red cardboard. Cherry sprinkled some more of their homemade "snow" on it. Then they put it at the foot of the tree and rigged up two big flashlights so that their beams played on the sign.

There was mistletoe, too, and colored crepe paper fished from somebody's trunk. The mess sergeant had had red- and green-iced doughnuts baked. There were flowers, sent from somebody's hothouse near by. The Red Cross people had lent games for the older children: ping pong, checkers, a book of guessing games.

"Not bad," the nurses agreed. "Not bad at all."

"Here's hoping the youngsters like it!"

"Now our last big job and then we'd better have lunch—"

The last job was wrapping the dozens and dozens of inexpensive little gifts which the nurses, pilots, and corpsmen had chipped in to buy for their small guests. The girls' gifts were wrapped in green paper, the boys' in red. The gifts were pitifully small—a roll of candy, a tiny doll, a toy watch. They were all that could be found in village shops, packages from home, foot lockers, and pockets.

The nurses and pilots, rather than disturb the party decorations, ate their lunch in the lounge, perched on the window sills and sitting on the floor.

CHRISTMAS PARTY   141

Wade, next to Cherry, told her that the corpsmen would be hosts to the children during the first part of the afternoon. Then the nurses and pilots would have their turn.

Cherry went back to the barracks and took a nap until it was time for the party. Most of the flight nurses followed suit. No one had any shame any more in admitting how severely nursing aloft tired them.

Toward the end of her nap, Cherry could have sworn someone was running a feather up and down her chin. She awoke to find the smallest flight nurse in captivity giggling beside her bed.

"Sleepyhead!"

"Lieutenant Grainger! How did *you* get here? You must have flown over in your C-47! Bring any patients?"

Muriel dimpled. "Mrs. Jaynes cycled me over. Merry Christmas! Here." She brought her hands from behind her back.

The other girls crowded around to see what Muriel had brought Cherry. It was one of Mrs. Eldredge's curious India cups. Cherry hardly felt she had a right to take it. But Muriel showed such dangerous signs of weeping that Cherry said hastily:

"Thank you very, very much! Whenever I drink out of it, I'll think 'Muriel gave me this!' "

The storm clouds disappeared from the small face. The child seemed to be waiting for something. She waited not only while Cherry changed into a fresh uniform, but she also kept silent until the last of the Flight Three nurses had departed.

She came over to Cherry, now that they were alone. "Want to see my father's Christmas gift to me?"

"I'd love to!" Cherry exclaimed. "But when was your father home?" she asked sharply.

"Mm—" Muriel had to stop and think. "It wasn't yesterday, nor the day before. Was it last week? Oh, yes, I remember. It was the day Lilac ate the worm."

Cherry said gravely, "Do show me your father's present."

Muriel hung back. "He said it is a very special secret present. And he said I have to wear it inside my dress, where no one can see it. Or else the charm won't work."

"Yes?"

"It's a lucky charm. And he said I mustn't show it to anyone."

"Then you must not show it to me."

Muriel looked disappointed. "But you're not just *anyone*. You're special too, just like this secret. Look!"

The little girl fumbled at the collar of her military blouse and drew out a ribbon. On it hung a sort of silver locket or medal. It was rather bent and nicked. A rose was outlined within a chased circle. On the back of the medal was stamped in Gothic script: "Berlin."

"What was the name of that song your father taught you?"

"*Röslein*. All about the lovely rose."

Lovely roses and lovely—spies! Cherry felt a little sick. She tucked the medal back in the child's blouse. "You'd better not show this to anyone else, dear, even though it is such a lovely present. To no one at all." In her excitement she had tensely grasped Muriel by the shoulders.

Muriel, sensitive to Cherry's troubled feelings, burst out:

"Do you think that my father is bad like the neighbors say?"

Here was the issue, and no evading it was possible.

Muriel looked up at her American aunt anxiously. Cherry drew the child onto her lap. "I think," she said slowly and deliberately, "that your father is a good man or he could not have such a lovely little daughter." She added silently, "And I believe that medal can be explained."

Maybe she was mad to think that, or sentimental. At any rate, there was no other attitude she could take with this bewildered little child.

"Don't show that medal to *anyone*," she warned Muriel once again. "It's very pretty, but keep your father's gift a secret. You promised him, remember. And now, let's go off to the party and enjoy ourselves!"

"Oh, let's enjoy ourselves!" Muriel cried eagerly.

Going in, they met Bunce coming out. He wore the broadest smile Cherry had ever seen on his blithe face.

Hanging on to both his hands were half a dozen small boys. His effort to salute Cherry was futile.

"We're goin' to see the plane!" Bunce said. "Yes, sir, these men are going to climb all over it."

"These men" were in too great a hurry to stop and chat. They tugged Bunce along, with small cries of "Going up, men!" and "Pip pip!"

"Have fun!" Cherry called to Bunce. He tucked two of the smallest boys under either arm and ambled off with the others trotting at his heels.

Muriel sniffed. "I don't like boys. They're dirty and they make too much noise."

"You'll feel differently when you're older," Cherry assured her. "Besides, don't you like Captain Wade?" she asked as she saw him coming. A small boy was riding on his shoulder.

But just then Muriel caught sight of the Christmas tree. She forgot herself, squeaked, and ran over to the tree, then wiggled her way through the group of excited children, closer to the tree. She dropped to her knees and gazed up at it rapturously.

"Is that candy?" she pointed hopefully at the decorations. A piece popped into her mouth completed her bliss.

Wade came over and knelt down, too, beside the tree. His small masculine passenger slid off the Captain's shoulder, made a horrible face at Muriel, and galloped off shouting.

Cherry looked through the pile of packages heaped at the foot of the Christmas tree, for something for the mascot. The mound of gifts had already grown smaller. Santa Claus Thorne appeared from behind the tree at that moment. Muriel's eyes popped.

"Saint Nicholas!" she whispered. "He *did* come!"

The jolly Santa leaned down to shake her hand and boom, "Merry Christmas!"

"Santa," Cherry said, "Muriel has been a very good girl, all this year. Have you a present for her, Santa?"

"Why, of course!" Santa enlarged upon all the gifts he and his trusty reindeer had brought. Cherry whispered to Muriel:

"What do you want?"

The small flight nurse was covered with confusion.

"Come on, tell us," Wade whispered.

"What I want—no. I'm a soldier now."

"I know what she wants, Santa," Cherry said. "A doll! Isn't that right?"

Muriel nodded. Cherry and Wade pinched and poked around in the packages until they found her a doll. It was only a rag doll but Muriel cradled it in her arms and pronounced it "beautiful." She thanked Santa, who turned to the next eager visitor.

"Captain Wade, I have another present," Muriel started, and her fingers strayed to the neck of her blouse. She caught Cherry's eye. Guiltily the small hand came down and awkwardly patted the doll.

"Don't I get to see your present?" Wade asked.

"This is a secret present," Cherry explained.

The thought of that medal, stamped Berlin, hanging around Muriel's baby neck, interfered with Cherry's enjoyment of the party. She helped organize a game of Going To Jerusalem, and took her turn at ladling out eggnog. But she was so absent-minded that several of her friends commented on it.

"You'll have to do better than this," Ann whispered to her. "After all, Lex's marriage surely couldn't hurt you so much!"

"It isn't—oh! Yes, Annie, you're right," Cherry evaded. "By the way, would you tell Gwen for me?"

Gwen, notified, came over to shake Cherry's hand.

"I never liked him," the redhead said flatly. "Whew! It's a relief to admit it."

"Kind of a relief to me too." Cherry grinned and wondered now why she had wept so hard this morning.

What an odd Christmas-birthday she was having. Other years, Cherry had been completely, light heartedly happy. This year, in England, came news from America—and hints of news from Berlin—that left her troubled.

"Hello, sobersides," said Wade, and yanked her black curls. "Cheer up. Don't you know this is your birthday party? Don't you know you're the glamour girl of this outfit? And don't you know your pal Muriel has suddenly become the guest of honor?"

A chorus of wobbly treble voices started to sing. Muriel's thin piping rose above the rest. Behind the children's carol, came the full-throated notes of a small portable organ, which one of the pilots had brought. Someone lit candles now. A hush came over the rest of the excited children as the little chorus sang. Then the organ pealed out familiar tunes, and everyone was singing. The voices, deep and high, blended and swelled, until the paper star atop the Christmas tree quivered.

Then Santa Claus read them *The Night Before Christmas* and Dickens' *Christmas Carol*. The small guests were half asleep, the smallest ones soundly asleep, by the time he finished. It was time to go home.

Cherry and Wade had assumed responsibility for taking home a dozen children in Muriel's village. Amid much confusion, they found the right coats, hats, scarfs, mittens and boots, and after a struggle, got each child buttoned and ready. Then into a jeep they went, tucked warmly under Army blankets. One little girl kept repeating sleepily, "Not even a mouse. Not *even* a mouse!"

The roads and lanes were pitch-black. Wade drove along carefully, this time, in the black-out. It seemed sad to Cherry that Christmas, most joyous of holidays, should ever have to be celebrated in the black shadows of war.

The last child but Muriel was taken home, and their jeep drew up before Mrs. Eldredge's wintry garden.

Muriel piped up, "Look! Someone left a light shining!"

Cherry and Wade followed the child's sleepy gaze. Yes, up there shone one bright light in the black-out. They had better black it out.

They climbed up a little hill, Wade and Cherry hand in hand, with the child tagging after them. They ran to turn the bright light out, running up and up to the very top of the hill.

The light, they found, was a star. It never could be blacked-out.

CHAPTER VIII

Under Fire

ONE AFTERNOON IN JANUARY, CHERRY WAS UNEXPECTedly called off hospital duty. Her name had not yet come up again, in the nurses' rotating roster of flight assignments. But she knew something was afoot. Across the field, a stockade of airborne infantry had been waiting restlessly for days, in one spot. They appeared to be alerted. High-ranking staff cars had been seen rolling around this Troop Carrier Command base. Whatever action was planned, it had been kept so secret there were not even rumors. Anyway, an emergency could hardly surprise Cherry any more.

She reported, as instructed, to a flight nurse from Flight One who was Captain Betty Ryan's assistant.

"Captain Ryan went out on a flight this morning," the nurse told Cherry. "I'll have to assign you myself.

This is an emergency mission. We're alerting a lot of our flight nurses. Don't discuss this order with anyone, please. Be down on the line in half an hour."

"Yes, Lieutenant." Cherry saluted. "Any flight plan to give me? Any information as to where we're going?"

"You'll learn that once you're up," the nurse said grimly. "Good luck."

Cherry raced over to the barracks and found every other girl in her flight—except Gwen, who was already out on a flight—alerted for the same mysterious mission. They pulled on their heaviest flying clothes—fur-lined jackets with parka hoods, heavy trousers, sheep-lined ankle boots—in tense silence. There was no time or use to speculate. Whatever was coming, it was something big and rough. The girls strapped on their pistols along with their musette bags.

At base operations hut, Cherry's flight team arrived just as she did. Wade made his clearances and the team headed for their aircraft. Cherry was amazed to see closely ranged inside the enormous hangar, great numbers of planes of all types, and even greater numbers of gliders.

"Wade, wh-what?—" she stammered in her excitement.

"Those are to carry infantrymen, and also tanks and field guns. They aren't starting for a few hours yet—not until we've gotten things ready for 'em."

"*We?* Oh, you mean we're hauling cargo to the front as usual."

"Just take a look at the cargo we're hauling today," Wade said grimly, as they approached their plane.

The doors of their enormous C-47 stood open. But instead of ammunition or gasoline or medical supplies being loaded aboard, soldiers were marching aboard. They were grave-faced, heavily armed infantrymen. In eleven other C-47's, more airborne infantry were filing aboard.

"Captain," Cherry asked, "aren't we going to pick up wounded today?"

"Certainly. But we're going to drop these men first. Aboard, please!"

Cherry, with Bunce right behind her, ran up the ramp into the plane. They slammed the doors shut, squeezed in, in the tail behind the soldiers, and strapped in. The plane's four motors roared, the aircraft vibrated, strained to lift. Cherry looked around curiously. The men, seated on the pull-down wall benches, were silent, tense. The very plane itself looked different. All her hospital equipment was stowed back close against the walls to make room for these men and their bulky tommy guns, parachutes, and field packs. It was evident they were going to be landed in enemy territory. Enemy territory! Cherry realized she was going to be in the thick of things today!

Their ship gave a terrific pull. The motors beat hard. Then they were taxiing, then swiftly taking-off. They gained altitude quickly. Before and behind them roared the other C-47's. Cherry looked out the low rear window. They were flying in two formations of six and six: each six spread out like two mutually protecting triangles.

"I've never seen this formation before," Cherry said to Bunce.

A soldier on her other side told her, "It's a combat formation, Lieutenant."

Cherry would have talked to this man, and those around him, but they were not communicative. Two or three of them had brief words of praise for a girl who would brave this work. One very young man said, with a grin, "Ma'am, when you get off this plane, the GI's just won't believe it. There'll even be wiseacres who'll point to your pants and say, 'No woman could possibly come here!' " Another said, "We're willing to dare anything so long as we know you medical people are near by."

A few words like these, and the men lapsed into silence. If they talked at all, they murmured to one another about fighting techniques, or about their families, or made grim jokes. One boy was reading his Bible. They were going into battle—going to be landed for a surprise attack to soften up the enemy, and open up the way for the other infantrymen who would follow.

No wonder, Cherry thought, that these young men sat grave and silent in the roaring plane.

She found it a long, tedious, nerve-racking trip. In these two hours, there were so many preparations she and Bunce needed to make for the wounded they were flying to pick up. But with the airborne GI's crowded aboard, it was impossible to pull down the web straps to hold litters, or get oxygen tanks or the sterilizer ready. Cherry and her medical technician did what they could in the tail, preparing medicines, bandages, and hot drinks. For the rest, they would simply have to wait till they landed, and then convert the transport from a carrier to a hospital plane at breakneck speed.

The south of England floated by below, gray and seemingly peaceful in the thin winter sunshine. Then their two formations were pounding over the Channel. Twenty minutes' hazardous flying over water, with an eye out for enemy planes, and then the coast of France hove into view. Here possibility of enemy attack, by planes and by flak from ground-based anti-aircraft guns, became very real. Here, too, their formation gradually split up and Cherry's plane flew alone. Now Wade gunned the motors to top speed.

Afternoon shadows were growing longer, over this unknown countryside. The soldiers glanced at their watches. Cherry began to recognize a few landmarks below, for this was her fifth combat mission. But they flew beyond the landmarks she knew, deep into fighting areas.

"Scared, Miss Cherry?" Bunce whispered.

"Who, me?" Then Cherry grinned. "Yes, plenty scared."

"I'm shakin' like a leaf."

"Never mind, we'll both put on a confidence act for our wounded."

She began to hear the rumble of heavy guns, louder and louder, as they streaked ahead. Sharp ack-ack sounded. A cloud of fiery spray shattered past their wing. Flak! Wade outflew that danger, got away fast from the German lines.

Cherry and Bunce strained their ears.

"Other planes?"

"I think so."

"Gosh, I hope they're ours."

"Aren't we nearly there *yet*?"

Bunce and Cherry kept watch at the window in the tail. Presently she pointed:

"Isn't that a camouflaged air strip?"

"But it's smack where they must be fighting! You can hear the guns real plain!"

Nevertheless, that was where Wade circled and started to go down. Cherry watched but saw no signal flags, nothing. Apparently all this had been arranged beforehand. There was nothing impromptu in the sure way their pilot set the plane down on this rough, mile-long strip, right in the middle of nowhere.

A few men in uniform came running down the air strip. Cherry could see no holding station, only a muddy clearing and clumps of broken trees. Planes and guns rumbled all around them. She distinctly saw flashes of fire, and smoke rising in the frosty air.

The infantrymen poured out of the plane. Cherry heard someone shouting "Nurse!" She located a doctor on the ground, waving to attract her attention.

"Nurse! There's no time to classify the wounded! You'll just have to pack 'em in as I send 'em to you. There're too many German planes around here!"

"Who's going to load, sir?" she yelled back.

"No trained teams here. We'll take anybody we can get!"

Hastily Cherry turned back into the plane with Bunce. While the last of the airborne infantry were still running out of the plane, she and Bunce started frantically to convert the plane to an ambulance ship. They snapped the benches back against the walls, pulled down the four litter straps to hold the tiers of stretchers, and opened the medical kit and hung it inside the plane door.

"Ready!" Cherry yelled to the Army field doctor, one minute later.

"Ready!" he relayed.

From the largest clump of bare trees, four soldiers picked up the first litter with its wounded man. They struggled through the wind and the gluey mud. Cherry held her breath lest they slip and drop the suffering man.

"Hurry!" the doctor urged them. Four more soldiers straightened up from the trees, bearing a second litter.

"Hurry, but *be careful*!" Cherry shouted to them.

There was an ominous roar far off in the sky. She looked up, saw nothing; looked back anxiously to the trees and saw walking wounded staggering toward the hospital plane. She bent over the first litter as it was carried up the rough gangplank to the open plane door. The man's tag read concussion and mental shock.

"Bunce! Have this case put up front where it's smooth riding. Here, fellow, take my hand," she said to an approaching ambulatory soldier with a bandaged head. "Go sit down. The sergeant will take care of you. All right, let's have that second litter! Hurry—but be careful! Don't jolt him!"

Litter-bearers and walking wounded struggled toward her through the mud. Above the pitiful procession, enemy planes soared into view. The Army doctor stared skyward anxiously, then shrugged and turned.

"Get that broken back case!" he yelled over the pounding of guns. "And this boy—" he ran to the trees.

Cherry classified the wounded as they came aboard, alone, without the doctor's help. She hoped he would give her a few instructions about them.

"Any special medicines I should get for these cases?" Bunce asked her.

"Where would you get medicine in this place?"

Suddenly a terrific crash broke out behind them. The whole sky seemed to darken with smoke. One of the soldiers carrying litters told Cherry:

"They're bombing our airfield half a mile away."

Cherry asked evenly, "We may be next?"

"We may."

"Put this hemorrhage case in a middle tier, where I can put a better tourniquet on him."

Wade suddenly appeared below the plane door, looking harassed.

"Where've you been?" Cherry called down. "Can you help load?"

"Sorry. Some of that flak just grazed us. We're still checking her over. What altitudes do you want?"

"Try to keep it eight thousand, not over. We have some bad head and chest cases that can't take it any higher. Wade! We're overloading. The doctor's making us take fourteen litters and seating all the ambulatories we can squeeze in, in the aisle."

"All right, throw out the men's baggage. But let's get upstairs before we get strafed."

As Wade turned away he collided with a man in torn civilian clothes. The man's sleeve was bloody.

"Sorry, old man," Wade apologized.

"Okay," the man said, in a passable American accent.

Cherry started. It was Mark Grainger!

Wade, completely unaware of the man's identity, ran back to the engines.

Mark Grainger boldly went up the ramp, as if to enter the plane.

"Just a minute," said Cherry, in a voice like steel. She blocked his way. "Let me see your medical tag."

If Mark Grainger recognized her, he showed not the faintest sign of recognition.

"I have no medical tag, but it's quite all right."

"Your credentials, then," Cherry challenged him. It hurt her to be hard with Muriel's father, with a man who was obviously wounded and suffering. But she was accountable for all patients who went aboard her plane.

Mark Grainger fumbled in his pockets as two more ambulatory patients climbed up the ramp leaning on the doctor.

"Hurry up! Get in!" the doctor warned. "Don't you hear those planes?"

The zoom of enemy planes was frighteningly closer now. Cherry waited a second until the doctor disappeared into the cabin, then turned again to Mark Grainger. He was holding out to her a sweat-stained visa.

The name on it was "Georges Lasalle." It bore a Belgian imprint.

"This won't do," Cherry said.

"You often take civilians," Mark Grainger countered.

They stared at each other, measuring each other, silently struggling.

"See here, your name is not Lasalle."

He looked worried and, in a dazed way, puzzled. Perhaps he did not recognize her, after all. Her face was smudged—he had seen her only once—he was dazed now from his wound—Cherry was so sorry for the injured man that, although each precious second counted, she gave him a hint.

"I know your little girl."

He hesitated. Cherry, her eyes fixed on his face, heard the roar of enemy planes in her eardrums. His expression was stony. Then his face cleared.

"You were at my house!"

"Yes."

He said low and rapidly, "I feel I can trust you. You must repeat this to no one, no one, you understand? I must get back to England. I don't care about my wound. I have a very important message that cannot be entrusted to the regular channels. You *must* fly me home!"

"Nurse!" said the exasperated doctor at her elbow. "You're holding things up. Come in here quickly while I give you instructions about these—Who's this man?"

"A casualty, sir."

"Where'd he come from? Has he a clearance? Or a priority?"

"He has a visa."

"You can't take an unknown civilian aboard simply because he has a visa!" Suddenly he shouted, "Come in here!"

But Cherry did not get under cover fast enough. German planes came swooping down, their guns firing, spitting hot steel; their shells whistling, bursting, crashing, making an inferno all around the planeful of wounded. Cherry looked straight ahead in horror. Four soldiers had just emerged from the trees with the last litter, to cross that muddy stretch of sudden death.

"Lie flat!" she screamed to them. "Lie flat!"

Mark Grainger seized her and pulled her inside the plane. The wounded were cowering, some crying from sheer excess of horror. Whistling bullets ripped into the mud all about the C-47, clipping one wing. Something up forward was on fire. Cherry tried to shout reassurance to her patients, but she could not make herself heard above the din.

The clamor suddenly grew deafening. The doctor cried, "Ours! Ours!"

Allied planes were driving the enemy planes away! U.S. Army ack-ack guns were opening up too.

Cherry stared around at the suffering men and shook with fury. To do this to helpless wounded! What an abomination that they had to suffer more terror before their initial agony could be relieved!

Bunce ran out into the smoke and noise and mud to the litter. He motioned to her joyously. All five men were all right. It was almost a miracle. Gently the wounded man was carried up the gangplank.

"The danger isn't over yet," the white-faced doctor said to Cherry. "You won't be safe anywhere over this area. Now, are they all in? Oh—that unknown civilian."

"I know him." Cherry said it in spite of herself. Mark Grainger was standing beside her and she felt him tremble. "I'll vouch for him."

"He's badly wounded," the Army doctor admitted. "But without clearance, you can't take him aboard. Besides, you're already overloaded."

"Sir, I'll assume full responsibility for taking him without permission," Cherry fought back.

The Army doctor frowned. "You're taking a long risk. You're doing it against regulations. Can't stand here arguing, though. I'll turn in a report on this man and you'll have to try to square yourself later. All right, now, watch that chest case for oxygen need, and give the amputation case blood plasma. Good luck!"

The doctor jumped down. Cherry had a sinking feeling of uncertainty as she watched Bunce pull the plane doors shut. If her faith in Muriel's father were misplaced, she would be in serious trouble.

Mark Grainger knew it, too. "Thanks," he whispered. "I'm sorry you re—"

Cherry flashed him a strange look. "Better sit down and strap in, now," she whispered quickly, as the plane started to roar. Then she took a deep breath and addressed the patients. "Men, we're going to go up now. You'll feel your ears cracking. I want you to keep swallowing. I'll be with you as soon as we level off."

The heavily crowded plane raced down the runway. Cherry and Bunce held their breaths, as if that somehow might make the plane lighter. Then they were off, rising steeply. Cherry breathed again. Only two fighter planes escorted them today. Couldn't more planes be spared?

She hurriedly picked her way along the jammed aisle. There were badly wounded men on those tiers of litters—facial wounds, a third degree burn, a broken back, a nerve injury, a nineteen-year-old boy whose feet had been frozen black and shriveled. Cherry worked as fast as she could with each one, cleansing, bandaging, giving strengthening blood plasma, germ-killing sulfa. She watched for oxygen need as their plane rose steadily higher. Why couldn't Wade stay around eight thousand feet? She motioned Bunce to give oxygen to two fainting men, and turned to treat the men seated on bucket seats and on the plane floor.

It was so crowded that when Wade bent to come through the cockpit door, he had to remain in the doorway. Cherry was surprised that he came at all, considering the danger of enemy planes.

Wade introduced himself to the patients and made his usual brief speech of reassurance. "Yes, sir, I've flown in tougher spots than this—Alaska, for example—"

In spite of her worry, Cherry had to grin. "Say, Captain," she called down the aisle, "I understand you flew in China? And Russia? And North Africa? And now in Alaska *too?*"

"That's right," Wade called back blandly. "Well, fellows, keep a stiff upper lip. We'll get you through safely. Nurse, come up here a second."

Cherry worked her way up to him. Wade drew her for a moment into the cockpit, out of the patients' hearing.

"What was that argument with the doctor? Anything wrong?"

"I took a wounded civilian aboard without full clearance."

"Who? What national?"

"I—it's sort of confidential—doesn't matter, anyway."

"I'm commander of this plane! Who is it?"

"All right, Wade. It's ... it's Mark Grainger."

Wade was so shocked he could only lean back against the closed cockpit door and stare at her.

"Holy cats! Now you *have* done it! A fine jam you've got yourself into! Suppose he's a—"

Cherry's hand flew up to Wade's lips, silencing him. "And suppose he isn't? You and I agree he might *not* be. Besides, what harm can he do aloft?"

"He could eavesdrop on what the wounded men are saying and pick up a lot of valuable information."

"Very well, Captain, I'll put him back in the tail all by himself."

"That's better. And when we land, you'll turn him right over to the authorities—just in case. Agreed?"

"Agreed, sir!"

Wade gave her a comforting pat on the shoulder, and Cherry went back to her patients. She immediately ordered her sergeant to place "that civilian" way back in the tail, alone, and give him first aid. She herself returned to the most severe casualties.

As always, the wounded followed her about with their eyes. One man on a top litter turned his head to whisper to their nurse:

"You're so pretty. You're the first pretty thing I've seen in months of ugliness."

"Thanks, soldier." Cherry stood on tiptoe. "I'll bet you have a pretty wife!"

"A lovely wife. Name's Ruth."

"Well, Ruth will be seeing you before long. Now I'll give you a sedative. I want you to try to sleep."

"All right." He swallowed the tablet, and obediently closed his eyes.

Cherry peered into a lower stretcher. A man with a burned, torn face stared back at her. He could talk, but did not want to talk. Cherry spoke gently to him, and carefully cleansed and swathed his face. She tucked the blanket around him. "Better now?"

He still did not reply but looked up at her tragically. "Soldier . . ."

"I don't want to live," he muttered. "I'm deformed."

"Soldier," Cherry said, "you do want to live. Plastic surgeons are going to restore your face. They will work from pre-war photographs of you. They'll turn you out as good as ever."

"You're not kidding me?"

"I am telling you the truth."

His lidless eyes filled with tears. "Okay."

"Do you believe me now?"

"Yes."

Right above him lay a young GI who had lost his right arm. He managed a smile for Cherry as she adjusted his pillow.

"Imagine finding a pretty girl here! Won't you stay and hold my hand?"

Cherry swallowed hard. That took courage—to flirt when he had just lost his arm. She took his left hand.

"You're quite a flirt, aren't you?" she smiled back. "You handsome boys always are."

"I—I *was* nice-looking before—until—"

"You're still mighty cute." Cherry swabbed the grime and sweat off his face. "You probably have three or four sweethearts."

"Nurse—Do you think girls will—will go out with me now?"

Cherry patted the soldier's cheek. "You're still *you*. That's what counts. How would you like some cool fruit juice?"

"Gee, Nurse, you make me feel lots better."

Most of the other patients were too badly hurt, or too dazed and faraway, to talk. Cherry went from one to another. Although she was thinking hard about the medical problem involved in each case, she noticed now that she heard only their own plane's engines. The fighter escort must have withdrawn. She noticed, too, as the air in here grew colder, thinner, harder to breathe, that their transport must be climbing again. Cherry hoped fervently it was not because there were enemy planes to avoid. This higher altitude aggravated certain cases. The usual nursing techniques did not work properly up this high. Cherry improvised as she went along, and also kept a sharp lookout to see which men needed more oxygen. Some of the sitting cases looked as if they might be airsick, though this was less important than their wounds. Cherry and Bunce tried to make them as comfortable as possible.

But her key job was to reassure these helpless men—particularly when, in back of them, came a roar, which steadily grew closer. Cherry counted. One—two—three—it sounded like three planes closing in on them.

Suddenly over the interphone came the copilot's voice:

"Three Messerschmitts at eleven o'clock! Came out of that cloud bank!"

Cherry picked up her own interphone and whispered into it furiously, "Turn off that radio back here! Do you want the men to hear?"

There was some buzzing and some talk back and forth. Wade's voice came over, "It's jammed."

The wounded men were alert and listening now.

Dick Greenberg, radioman and navigator, spoke next:

"S O S. S O S. C-47 hauling wounded—approaching Cologne. Want fighter protection. Over."

Up front a gun went off with a terrific bang. The Germans were trying to get the pilot or the C-47's engines. The suffering men in the litters were pale and sweating, their eyes distended.

"S O S. C-47 approaching Cologne. Fighter protection. Urgent."

Their ship lurched and rolled sideways. Everyone not taped into litters was thrown. Cherry got to her feet, feeling a pain in her back, but with her attention fixed on a casualty who was growing hysterical. She gave him a hypodermic. Now, if ever, was the time to keep her head. Bullets whistled, and engines roared outside the plane.

"S O S—C-47 hauling wounded—fighters, fighters. Come in!"

The noise outside nearly split their eardrums.

"S O S—fighters—"

Then a strange voice asked, "What the heck do you think we are?" Past the rear window flew a group of Allied fighter planes.

A distinctly British voice said, "Cheer up, chickens, we have you."

The wounded cheered. Some wept, and Cherry all but wept too. They could hear the air battle shrieking outside.

American Mustangs and British Spitfires fought off the Messerschmitts. They drove them away quickly. Wade rode steady through it all.

Then, flying lower and slower, the fighters mothered the big transport across France, and all the way to the Channel.

Cherry had soothed her patients by this time, and helped the worst shocked over their violent reactions.

There was order and quiet in the ambulance plane once more, so now Cherry could relax a little. She noticed that her back pained and that she was limping, but she went right on cauterizing a bad wound, happy in the thought that they would soon be home. At last, they were safely over the Channel! Below them, in the waning sunlight, stood the cliffs of England!

Only an hour more, in safe skies. Cherry checked their Estimated Time of Arrival, sent radio notification of the number of wounded aboard and asked to have extra ambulances waiting. Only an hour more, but it was still a long, hard pull. Cherry realized now that their aircraft was shot up and that Wade was bringing them in largely on sheer skill and will power. Wade sent back a message by Bill Mason.

"We're a mess of holes, but tell the boys 'Papa's going to take you home.'"

And he did. They flew low over their home base at dusk. She looked down on the field to see the ambulances and unloading crews and ground crews waiting. The entire complement of the field, and a crowd of pilots and flight nurses, were standing all over the field, looking up for their C-47! Cherry thought of all the times she had sweated in overdue or imperiled planes. Now she was being sweated in herself! The radioman must have notified home base of the air battle over Germany.

They circled past the control tower, and skimmed lower and lower over the runway. Cherry could see the uplifted faces clearly, now, in the January twilight. They were strained and anxious. She and Bunce prepared the wounded to be moved, then strapped them down firmly for the landing. She kept an eye on Mark Grainger as their wheels touched the air strip. Mark Grainger was to be turned over to the military police immediately.

As they skidded perilously to a stop, ground crewmen swarmed to the transport. The ambulances waiting at the runway backed up to the plane doors. Major Thorne tugged them open as Cherry and Bunce pushed from inside, and the cold air poured in. They were home—safe and out of danger. They were home! Cherry saw the American flag fluttering down from the hospital flagpole. Nothing had ever before looked so good to her as that familiar red, white, and blue.

"Lieutenant Ames! Are you all right?" demanded the Flight Surgeon. She nodded, and he asked, "What cases have you brought?"

Cherry rapidly led him through the plane, and also handed him a brief report on each patient. She signaled the unloading crew to come aboard. Promptly, under her supervision and with Bunce's help, they lifted two litters at a time onto the hydraulic elevator. More loaders on the ground swiftly put the men on stretchers into the ambulances. The Flight Surgeon was already detailing the worst injured for immediate operations.

Wade called from the ground, "All right, Lieutenant?"

"Yes, Captain. Are you?"

"Yes." Wade nodded in an exhausted way. He was too tense, too full of battle, to talk yet. He strode off to direct the mechanics, who had waited weary anxious hours for their endangered plane. Then Cherry saw him go off toward the base operations hut.

She was helping the walking wounded off the plane when Captain Betty Ryan ran up beside her.

"Lieutenant Ames, I've been so worried about you! Why, you're limping!"

The Flight Surgeon turned to look. "It's your back, isn't it?"

"I was thrown," Cherry confessed. "It's nothing. Was everyone taken care of all right, sir?"

"You did a magnificent job," Major Thorne said. "I'm officially going to commend you for what you did on this combat flight! Don't you think she deserves it, Captain Ryan?"

"Lieutenant Ames fully deserves it," the Chief Nurse said warmly. "Thank heavens those Mustangs and Spitfires showed up!"

Cherry glowed. She felt her tiredness draining away, and in its place, a deep well-earned satisfaction. She honestly felt that on this terrible flight—this great test—she had fully lived up to her nurse's idealism. She had brought the wounded home and given them care, in spite of all odds. Suddenly Cherry remembered Mark Grainger. She would have serious explanations to make! She had broken military regulations.

"Excuse me," she said to her two superior officers, "I have to go back to the plane."

"Just a minute." Plump Major Thorne wiggled his finger at her. "I want you to report to the hospital and have that back looked at."

"In fact," said Captain Ryan slowly, "I think you'd better have a complete physical checkup. I've had my eye on you for some time, Lieutenant Ames, and I'm not at all pleased with that tired look of yours. I even thought we ought to ship you home one of these days for a good, long rest."

"Oh, no!" Cherry wailed. "You can't do that to me! Why, these big battles are just starting—you need every flight nurse—oh, no! I don't want to miss anything!" Then suddenly she remembered Mark Grainger again.

"If you'll excuse me—"

She limped back to the tail. Mark Grainger was not there. She hunted furiously through the plane. He was not there. Out on the field, she searched frantically among the ambulances. She saw no one in civilian clothes. She questioned the loaders. No one remembered seeing a civilian. She ran, despite her twinging back, a little distance around the plane, then up the runway. In the gathering dusk, only figures in khaki or in blue fatigues came to meet her.

Mark Grainger had disappeared! Slipped away!

"Now I am in for it! If he's a spy—and I've let him get away after I've illegally brought him into the country—Oh, my heavens, what have I done!"

She thought of something else. Mark was wounded. Bunce had given him only first aid. If he were a spy—and would not dare call a doctor—infection, worst danger of any wound, might set in.

He might easily be found at Mrs. Eldredge's. He might call a local doctor. But that did not remove Cherry's guilt. Catching a criminal does not clear an accessory to the crime.

Cherry stood still on the busy, darkening field. She pressed both hands to her throbbing temples.

"So I'm in danger of going home for a rest, am I? I only wish it were merely that! *Spy or not*—when the military police learn what I've done, I'll be sent home, all right—dishonorably discharged!"

Frightened, but determined to face the consequences, Cherry went to General Headquarters and reported in detail to the Commanding Officer. She was warned not to talk about the situation to anyone. In the meantime, she was to go on with her duties until further notice.

CHAPTER IX

The Mystery Explained

CHERRY WAS NOW SOMETHING OF A HEROINE. THE OTHER Flight Three nurses had had their adventures, too, but none so hair-raising as Cherry's. Upon this they agreed.

Later that week, as the six girls rested in their barracks room, Lieutenant Gray said, "Imagine coming face to face with an enemy plane! How I would have loved that!"

"You would not," Gwen contradicted her. "Sounds thrilling to hear about, but boy, I'll take my thrills on a roller coaster, or something nice and safe!"

"Weren't you thrilled, Cherry?" the energetic New Englander insisted.

Cherry ruefully shook her black curls. "I was scared to a jelly. I shook like a jelly too."

Ann poked her here and there with one finger. "You seem to have hardened into your normal consistency again."

"She still looks as if she saw a ghost!" Elsie Wiegand declared.

"Well, she has a right to look like a jelly or a ghost or *anything!*" little Maggie defended her. "Cherry did one of the bravest—"

"Hear, hear!" Cherry waved a handkerchief over her head like a flag. "Good heavens, kids, can't we talk about something else? The weather, for instance?"

"Well, you *are* a heroine. And," Ann pointed out, "you brought it on yourself."

Cherry thought, "If you only knew what else I've really brought down on my head!" She fully and soberly expected the military police to summon her any minute. Wouldn't the girls be disappointed in their 'heroine' then?

Cherry's reaction to her narrow escape in the air surprised her. She found that she was writing long letters home—thinking of home in a new, homesick way. Like all soldiers, Cherry and the other nurses constantly talked and thought of home. Yet they would not have gone home if Headquarters had told them they could. Now home seemed to Cherry more real than the nightmare she had just lived through. Her mother, Midge, their big gray house in Hilton, seemed closer and more real than the Army people and English countryside which Cherry could reach out and touch. It comforted her to talk with them by writing letters. She was careful, though, to omit any mention of her fatigue and her strained back.

Cherry reported to the hospital for her checkup. When the doctor and the attending nurse saw her bright eyes and cherry-red cheeks, they declared:

"*You* sick? We don't believe it."

"I'm out of order," Cherry insisted. "But not much."

After they had examined her, the doctor and nurse laughingly told her they had to apologize. "You are out of order, at that."

"May I see my health report?" Cherry requested.

But they refused. Cherry was puzzled, and a little uneasy, about that. However, it could not be helped, and what good was worrying? So she dismissed the matter. Besides, she felt very much better now. Even her limp was wearing off.

"Too bad," she joked to the other girls. "That limp was so picturesque!"

"We could toss you down a flight of stairs, if you'd like," Gwen offered. "Always co-operative."

Cherry refused with thanks.

Flight Three was having a sort of holiday. Under orders to rest, the girls' only obligations, temporarily, were drill and calisthenics and road marches. Cherry had time now to stand out on the windy airfield with Wade

THE MYSTERY EXPLAINED 177

Cooper and wait for their pilot friends to come roaring home. If the sound of outgoing bombers and fighters had haunted her before, they very nearly stopped her breathing now. For she herself had been through an air battle. She knew vividly what those young men went out to face, and what they would—or would never—return from. When Shep or Tiny or Bob came down wide open and screaming to "buzz" the field, nearly sweeping the ground, or joyously did roll-overs, Cherry really shared their elation now.

"Wade," Cherry asked, "how can those pilots keep going right back into combat?"

"I did it," he said indignantly, "until they made a nursemaid out of me!"

Cherry chuckled. "Still griping! But seriously, do you mean to say that, after the dose we had the other day, you *want* more of the same?"

"Sure. That's my job. Not this namby-pamby—"

"We know, we know," Cherry said hastily. "But haven't you any fear? Any nerves? The other boys do. What are you made of, anyway, Wade Cooper?"

Wade grinned. " 'Snails and nails and puppy dogs' tails,' " he quoted the old rhyme. "Why, I was mortified the other day! There I was without a gun, and some fighters had to rescue me. Rescue *me*—as if I were an old lady!"

Cherry looked into his lively brown eyes with real curiosity. "You mean to stand there and blithely tell me you weren't scared when those Messerschmitts came to call?"

"Shucks, no! I wasn't scared. I was mad. All I could think was, 'If a bullet breaks the plexiglass nose and lets the below-zero air rush in, I'm going to be one mad pilot!'"

"Well, I was scared," Cherry announced.

"Well, you're a sissy," Wade, joking, glanced at her sideways, then put his arm about her shoulders. "Cherry, I'll tell you something. I'm asking for a transfer back to combat flying."

For a moment Cherry could not speak. She hated to think of Wade going back into combat. But he looked so eager, he wanted her approval so much.

"That's fine, Wade," she made herself say cheerfully. "I hope you get it."

"Spoken like a real sport! Cherry, pal, if and when I get a nice new bomber, I'm going to name it after you. Going to paint your picture on the side—black eyes, black curls, red cheeks, and all." He squinted at her appreciatively. "Maybe I'll have 'em paint a bunch of red cherries in your hair."

"That'll be great, just great," Cherry said weakly.

Well, she had not convinced Wade that flying the ambulances was for him. Apparently it was really not for him, or he would not have had this persistent urge to return to combat flying. If that was what he really

THE MYSTERY EXPLAINED 179

had his heart set on, then Cherry, too, wished for his transfer to come through.

They talked about it at the dance that night, which the Red Cross was giving in the recreation hall. Some black soldiers, just returned from fighting in Italy, volunteered to supply the dance music. Those soldiers were just about the hottest band Cherry had ever heard, beating it out with their whole hearts. It was the first real swing heard at this base in England, and everybody perked up. Cherry was having a wonderful time dancing with the pilots. She was in no mood to talk seriously, or talk at all, with that trumpet wailing plaintively and the drums flirting with the rippling piano.

But Wade wanted to talk. Besides, Wade kept stepping on her feet. Captain Cooper was a better pilot than dancer. Out of courtesy to him, and also out of regard for her feet, Cherry suggested they sit this number out. They perched on a table beside the band.

Wade was full of hope for transfer back to combat flying. But he was worried about one thing. He was worried about what might happen to Cherry for arranging Mark Grainger's passage.

"Have you heard anything, Cherry?"

"No, I'm waiting—waiting pretty anxiously."

"You still feel this man may be innocent?"

Cherry said stubbornly, "In spite of everything—yes."

"Well, heaven help you if he isn't innocent."

Perhaps the music lightened her worry. Or perhaps that faith she had clung to all these months came to her rescue now. At any rate, Cherry laughed and said, "Heaven isn't going to rescue me! This is one time when I'll have to clear myself, *by* myself. Or would you care to rescue me, Captain Cooper?"

"I'd do most anything for you, and you know it. Jeepers, Cherry, if I do get transferred out of this work, I'm going to be mighty sorry to say 'so long' to you. Maybe we could—maybe we—uh—"

The dauntless pilot, faced with making a romantic speech, crimsoned and stuttered.

"Yes, yes, go on," Cherry teased him.

"I—uh— That is—you and I— We've been good pals. So maybe—" Wade broke down altogether. "How'd you like a Coke?" he asked desperately.

Cherry, frankly laughing by this time, settled for a Coke.

Cherry did not feel lighthearted next day when she received word to go to Mrs. Eldredge's house. Elsie had taken the message for her over the phone. Cherry cross-questioned her: who had called? what sort of voice was it? exactly what was said? where had the call been made from?

"I don't know all that," Elsie said rather impatiently. "It was a man's voice, and he said would you please be at that address this evening. Gracious, Cherry, from

THE MYSTERY EXPLAINED 181

the fuss you're making, you'd think it was Scotland Yard calling you, or something!"

Cherry found that a pretty grim joke, under the circumstances. She immediately secured time off for that evening, from the Chief Flight Nurse, and worried herself through an endless day of debating whether she should report the mysterious phone call to Headquarters at once, or whether she should still follow her intuitive belief in Mark. Perhaps this visit tonight would disclose his innocence. By the time evening and the hour for her visit had arrived, she was badly upset. But she had made up her mind not to report it. She had a strong feeling that tonight she would learn the truth.

All the way over to the village, bouncing in an Army truck, Cherry's anxiety mounted. What would this evening bring? Would she learn whether her faith in little Muriel's father was or was not justified?

The soldier-driver let her out on blacked-out High Street, and she hurried through the darkened lanes alone. At Mrs. Eldredge's garden gate, she paused. The icy bushes and trees looked like fantastic figures threatening her. But Muriel's voice beyond the heavily curtained windows reassured her. Cherry went up the path and knocked on the blue door.

Mrs. Eldredge admitted her without a word, then bolted the door. A curious silence fell as Cherry entered. Here was the familiar, lovely room, with a warm fire leaping in the fireplace. Here were the India cups on the sideboard—the inviting chairs—the clock ticking—everything was the same. Then why was the atmosphere so changed?

Mark Grainger, wrapped in blankets, and with his arm in a sling, was sitting beside the fire. On a little footstool beside him, sat Muriel, adoration in her thin face. Even Lilac, at her feet, was still. Cherry looked around in dread for other people—military police, British Intelligence, or American Army officials. But there were only the four friends in this quiet room.

Mark broke the uncanny silence. "Come in, Miss Ames, and sit down. You sit down too, please, Mother Eldredge. I have a great many things to say to you both."

Muriel whispered loudly to her father, "May I say hello to Aunt Cherry now?"

Mark whispered back loudly, with a smile. "Yes, but not too much noise. This is a confidential meeting, remember."

Muriel leaped off her footstool and landed in Cherry's lap. Lilac also clambered all over her.

"My father's home! Isn't that wonderful? Even Lilac is glad."

"I'm glad for you, too," Cherry said. "Are you taking good care of your father's arm?"

"Oh, yes." Muriel nodded gravely. "I'm a nurse, aren't I? You know what? The doll Saint Nicholas gave me—

she's going to be a nurse, too, when she gets big enough."

"How is your doll?"

"She's well, thank you, except for a slight sniffle. Lilac licked off her complexion."

They were all smiling now. Mrs. Eldredge walked over to Muriel and held out her hand. "Time for sleep, dear."

Muriel wailed. It was earlier than her usual bedtime.

Her father said pleasantly, "Grandmother and Miss Cherry and I have grown-up things to talk over. I would consider it real co-operation on your part if you said good night now, like a good child."

"Good night," chirped Muriel promptly. Grabbing Lilac's collar, she planted a kiss on her father's ear and skipped off to bed.

Cherry and Mark Grainger chatted, stiffly, while Mrs. Eldredge put Muriel to bed.

"Is your arm improving?"

"Yes, thanks. It wasn't too bad. I can't believe our enemy could keep an Englishman down permanently! And our local physician is very competent."

"I—er—was wondering how you got home from the air base the other day, in your weakened condition."

Mark Grainger coolly settled into his chair. "I thumbed my way, as you Americans say, in a jeep. Sorry to have strolled out on you without offering my thanks. I was rather in a hurry."

"I can imagine," Cherry said dryly.

"With that urgent report, you know."

"No, I don't know!"

"Well, here is Mother Eldredge. I'll start at the beginning."

The three of them pulled their chairs closer together in front of the fireplace, for this conversation was not to be overheard by any passers-by. Cherry saw how taut and anxious the elderly woman was. Cherry herself was waiting tensely for what might be coming. She was determined to listen to whatever Mark Grainger would say, both with good will and a critical ear for lies.

His very first words, delivered with conviction and offered with proof, filled her with relief.

"I am not a spy. I am not working for the Germans. I am working for Britain, for the Allied cause, in the British Intelligence—and have been all along. Here is proof." He rose, and with difficulty reached behind the clock. He brought out a letter and showed it to them. The letter, indubitably authentic and signed by two high personages, confirmed what he said. Mark Grainger sat down again, smiling now.

Cherry and Mrs. Eldredge could only gasp.

"But, Mark," Mrs. Eldredge said in amazement, "what could have been your reason to keep silent while all those horrible charges were being made against you?"

Mark Grainger smoothed his blond hair. "When I tell you the whole story, you will see why I needed,

THE MYSTERY EXPLAINED 185

and still need, to keep silence. Why I am unable to defend myself against cries of 'Spy!' I am telling you only because Miss Ames has jeopardized her military standing, though I am also glad to have this opportunity to relieve your mind, Mother Eldredge. Please understand that you must keep this secret, for my work must go on."

Mrs. Eldredge and Cherry both promised.

"You know that in the countries the Germans have occupied—France, Belgium, Holland, Poland, parts of Russia, Norway, Denmark, Czechoslovakia, Austria, Greece—there are brave people who will not submit to Germans coming into their countries and ruling them. You also know that if patriots were to defy their invaders openly, they would be shot, and so would not be able to accomplish anything against the enemy. So they have to resist the Germans secretly.

"On the surface they seem to obey. But secretly they have organized an underground. It is extremely dangerous, as you can imagine. This underground does work of the greatest importance to the Allied armies—supplies information about the enemy that helps us win battles. And, of course, our winning battles means that we will be able to drive the Germans out of the occupied countries, and free these people to rule themselves."

"I understand," Cherry murmured.

"My work is with the underground," Mark Grainger explained. "You know that I am an engineer. I also happen to speak German and French, fluently. So I was assigned to Belgium, to get in touch secretly with Belgian patriots working for the underground. My task was to learn such things from them as—well, I cannot tell you in much detail. But here are some examples: I was to learn, under the noses of the Germans in Belgium, where the German robot bomb factories were hidden, so that our bombing planes could blow them up. Sometimes, too, we would smuggle out captured Allied soldiers, so they could fight again. Or sometimes we would secretly bring a Belgian into England, train him in intelligence work, and take him back to work for his underground."

"Fantastic," Mrs. Eldredge said. "Fantastic."

"The whole war is fantastic," Mark replied. "The idea of so-called civilized people killing off one another is fantastic, isn't it?"

Cherry's mind was teeming with questions. She hardly knew where to start. "But how did you get from England to Belgium without the enemy knowing?"

"By Army plane. I dropped into German-occupied Belgium by parachute, at night, usually, to lessen the chance of being caught. Sometimes I would wear a uniform and on occasion I would wear civilian clothes."

Suddenly to Cherry's mind came vividly the picture of Mark Grainger, dressed in shabby civilian clothes, furtively loitering around the special plane.

"So that's why I once saw you loitering about a plane on that air strip!" Cherry blurted out.

Mark started. "You saw me? Recognized me? And you didn't report me?"

"No, I did not report you then. I gave you the benefit of the doubt."

The young man leaned back in his chair once more. "Thank heavens for that! If you had spoken, you might have undone months of perilous work. When you saw me, I had just come in by plane. I was trying to get away unnoticed, for not even Army people could know my work. Thank you, Miss Ames. Thank you for having had some faith in me."

"But, Mr. Grainger," Cherry started to say when Mrs. Eldredge began to weep softly. "Oh, Mark! Oh, Mark!" she cried, "it was hard to have faith in you at times. Those telephone calls in German—your visitors in the middle of the night—and then that note—"

"I realize your position, Mother Eldredge," Mark said gently. "Believe me, I never once felt any reproach toward you for your suspicions. What else could you think? We had to use German, here in England, to keep our English neighbors from learning our work. You know how gossip spreads, and this work *must* be kept secret! If we had used English in England, people would have understood; if French, they could have guessed. No, we had to use German to put them off the scent. By the way, I was amused when the neighbors reported me to Scotland Yard. I've been working with Scotland Yard. Naturally the neighbors received no answer when they reported me. But it hurt when they made my little girl feel that—being loyal to her father was wrong."

Mrs. Eldredge twisted her veined hands. "I'm afraid that I, too, made the child unhappy by my suspicious attitude."

Mark reached over and gave her a reassuring pat on the hand. Then he turned his handsome, strong face to Cherry. "And, Miss Ames," he smiled gently, "I realize your position, too, it was your duty to report me when you did."

Cherry was startled.

"So General Headquarters has contacted you?" Cherry asked.

"Yes, Miss Ames. Your Commanding Officer knows all the facts on the case." Cherry felt some sense of relief. At least it was established that Mark was not a spy; that he was doing invaluable work for the Allies. But it did not clear her part in the situation, she knew. She had broken regulations, and she would be punished. Mark continued, "I'm indebted to you, Miss Ames, for all you have done, and for reassuring Muriel and protecting her. You softened her troubles for her. I know of no way to tell you what that means to me. I am in your debt for a great deal! For bringing me home the other day—"

"How did you usually return from Belgium to England?"

"As best I could. Sometimes it was possible to make arrangements beforehand, sometimes I simply had to rely on my wits and luck. You realize I could not just get aboard any Allied plane, for no one except a high Intelligence officer was to know my identity and work. And it is not always possible, in battle, to locate the highest-ranking Intelligence officer for clearance. I did not dare carry any valid written identification, no written messages—nothing. All the information that I secured had to be memorized and kept locked in my head. If I had been caught, you see, with written proof, not only I, but innocent people in the underground would have been shot."

They sat for a moment brooding over his danger-filled existence.

Cherry asked hesitantly, "May I ask how you knew which people were members of the underground?"

Mark laughed a little. "Since we have now changed the method, I can tell you. Well, in the first place, no underground worker ever knows more than two or three other members. So that, in case one is caught, he or she *cannot* possess much information to be tortured out of him. Few of them ever talk, anyway. In these last few months, I worked with two men and a woman. Belgians. Just everyday people like you and me, who loved their country and wanted to get the Germans out of it. There were Germans everywhere in Belgium. We had to have some sort of signal which the Germans would not suspect. So we agreed we would whistle or sing an old, familiar German song, under the enemy's very nose."

"The song Muriel sang for me? *Röslein*?"

"Yes. Perhaps I was indiscreet to teach her that song, but it—it meant so very much to me."

"It meant your life," Mrs. Eldredge said simply.

"And the silver medal with the rose?" Cherry asked. Mark Grainger's face clouded. He seemed to be seeing another land, other scenes. "That medal had its part in saving my life. The woman underground member gave it to me—partly to augment the song signal and identify me to someone in a new area of Belgium where I was going, partly as a good luck piece. I got safely into the new territory, but the Germans picked me up. It looked bad for me. But because I had in my possession this medal stamped Berlin, which only a pro German was likely to own—since it was an old and typically German school trophy—I could say I had gone to school in Germany, and they let me go. It really turned out to be my good luck charm, you see."

"And you gave it to Muriel," Cherry said softly.

Mark Grainger's brow furrowed. He talked into the fire. "It had kept me safe. I felt that perhaps it would keep her safe, too, from the robot bombs. And besides—If I had never come back, I wanted Muriel

THE MYSTERY EXPLAINED 191

to have something of her father. I wanted her to have some sign, even if she did not understand it, of what her father had been doing."

"She will know, some day," Mrs. Eldredge said in a choked voice, "that her father was no spy but the bravest of patriots!"

Mark smiled wryly. "Until that day comes, I will have to go on permitting my name to be blackened. Muriel will continue to hear only bad of me. She must simply have faith in her father."

Cherry leaned forward to him. "I think she will."

They smiled at each other.

Cherry said eagerly, "Could we bring her in and tell her a little of this—just a little—to relieve her worry, and yours."

Mark Grainger stood up. "Yes! Yes! You're right. I'll get her."

He came back leading the sleepy child by the hand. She was rosy from sleep and smiled vaguely at Cherry. Mark sat down and held her on his lap.

"You tell her, Miss Cherry. You've kept up her faith in me so far."

Cherry took Muriel's small warm hands in her own.

"Can you keep a very big secret? For your father's safety?"

Muriel nodded, wide-eyed.

"Well, here's the secret. No matter what anybody says against your father, I know, and your grandmother knows, and you know—that it isn't true! We must not say so now. But after the war is over, everybody will find out Muriel's father is a real hero."

Muriel blinked sleepily. "I always thought he was a hero anyway. But you mean, when Mr. Heath says my father is 'no good'—or Tony and Meg say he's a spy—it isn't true?"

Her grandmother said emphatically, "It absolutely is not true!" She added, "But we still have to pretend we don't know anything about it."

Muriel heaved a great sigh. "Oh, I'm terribly glad. I never b'lieved those mean things about you, Father, but sometimes Lilac and I felt quite hurt. I guess we won't any more. Just pretend, mm? Just pretend."

She was smiling happily and clinging to her father's hand as he led her back to bed. When Mark Grainger returned, they conversed a little longer. Cherry asked Mark Grainger why he had chosen this perilous work.

"Why did you choose to become a flight nurse?" he countered, laughing. "That isn't precisely a safe or easy job."

Cherry smiled back. "Oh—I don't exactly know. I've long since forgotten I had a choice to make. Feels now as if I'd been chosen."

"That's how I feel."

"I've never experienced such satisfaction as comes from helping a soldier through his suffering."

Mark nodded. "Or helping brave, persecuted people fight for their freedom."

Mrs. Eldredge really smiled, for the first time that quietly momentous evening. "You two are rather two of a kind, aren't you?"

Cherry rose to go. Mark Grainger offered to see her at least as far as High Street but she refused because he was still weak. Good-byes were said, and the British family's thanks proffered again.

"Come back to England after we've chased the Jerries away," they called after Cherry as she went down the path. "Then we'll really repay you."

Cherry waved, and shut the gate. She took what was to be her last look at that almost enchanted white cottage.

CHAPTER X

Mission Home

"GET UP! WAKE UP!" ANN WAS LAUGHING AND SHAKING them. "Wake up this minute!"

The Flight Three girls rolled out wearily. In the men's long, woolen GI underwear which they wore these cold months as pajamas, they were a sight to behold.

"It's not six A.M. yet," Cherry groaned.

Gwen was sitting up with her eyes shut. "Ann, how can you do this to me?"

Ann, fully dressed and awake, ripped Aggie's covers back. "Get up! Jack arrived half an hour ago! And he's already got permission and we're to be married today! Get up and help the bride!"

"Hurray for you!" Cherry cried. "Hurray for love!" She bounced off her bed and seized the other girls' hands. They danced in a circle around Ann, shouting, "Annie's get-ting mar-ried! Annie's get—"

Ann waved her arms at the five crazy dancing figures in oversize long underwear.

"Will you loons control yourselves and *help* me? I haven't a wedding dress—we haven't any place to spend a honeymoon—no ring—no refreshments—" Ann's face changed. "Why, nobody's even invited yet! Hey, kids, nobody even *knows* I'm getting married!"

From the adjoining barracks rooms on all sides came muffled shouts from the other flights.

"We know it! Think we're deaf? Congratulations!"

"You're making enough noise to wake up a dead man in Chicago! But we forgive you!"

"Are we invited to the wedding? Say yes!"

Ann, excited and flushed, shouted back with most unaccustomed lack of dignity. "'Course you're invited! All of you! It's this afternoon!"

The five assorted imps in long underwear burst into song and dance again, around the bride. Other sleepy nurses rushed in, too. Bedlam, itself, seemed to have broken loose in the barracks.

If Cherry had any secret sorrows about the trouble she was in, she drowned those sorrows in the girls' mad scramble to arrange Ann's wedding. First they put Ann to bed to rest. Then they went to call on the groom—shy Jack Powell, quiet and blue-eyed as Ann herself. Jack had wisely taken himself out of the way of these stampeding females. He had gone off to see the chaplain to ask him to officiate. Cherry left a note at Jack's barracks, which all the nurses signed:

Here comes the groom,
Fresh to his doom—
Look at the crease
In his new pantaloon!

Next stop was a wedding gown for Ann. They held a hurried consultation. "White—white—what the dickens around here is white?" Gwen puzzled.

"Bed sheets," little Maggie supplied. "I saw a lovely new one in a ward supply closet the other day. It had a sheen like silk, 'cause it's brand-new."

Cherry looked at Aggie and Elsie. "Well, stylists? If I can wangle the sheet out of the ward, will you drape and tack it into a wedding gown for Ann?"

Aggie pretended to roll up her sleeves. "Just go get it, Ames!"

Elsie was already figuring. "If it's regulation size, she can even have a train. A veil—a veil, kids—we have nothing but next summer's mosquito netting—"

"Starch it and double it," Gwen replied. "Make a short flyaway net veil. See? And over it, a crown of fresh flowers."

"And a bouquet!" they chorused. "Ought to be white flowers."

"I'll go pick 'em," Gwen volunteered. "Off the wards." She put on her most demure expression, a sure sign she was up to mischief, and vanished in the direction of the hospital.

"Ann's going to look like something by the grandest *couturier* or I'll eat my medical kit," Aggie Gray vowed. "C'mon, Elsie!" Off they went, too, to start on the bride's veil.

"Food," Cherry said to little Maggie. "You and me're left —and left with that problem."

"Food for the wedding guests," Maggie echoed worriedly. "And then decorate the chapel. With what, though?"

"Fir boughs?" Cherry suggested vaguely. "And oh, yes! We must get that nurse from Flight Two to do Ann's hair and nails."

"Have you any chocolate bars? With almonds? To pay her with, I mean."

When they hunted up the nurse, she delightedly refused any chocolate bars and dashed away to make the bride beautiful. Cherry and little Maggie hurried off to see the Mess Officer.

"What do you suppose we have here in Britain?" he said. "The same old thing you've been eating for weeks. Mutton."

The two nurses groaned. Then Cherry observed:

"Mutton's better'n nuttin'. Can we have a nice mock-chicken salad or sandwiches, or something? And coffee?"

"You bet," the Mess Officer promised. "I'll disguise that mutton so its own mother wouldn't recognize it. I'll get you a wedding cake baked, too. We'll have the reception in Officers' Mess hall. If you nurses and pilots don't get any lunch today, blame it on Cupid."

They thanked him fervently, and sped off to plead for—and win—the satiny new sheet. Back to the barracks, Cherry and Maggie flew with their treasure. Then off to the chapel, to see what could be done there. Cherry gratefully found the Flight One nurses already making the chapel festive with garlands of glossy dark rhododendron leaves. Flight One had even pressed their pilots into service as a corps of ushers.

"Gosh!" said Cherry in awe-struck tones. "Even in the Army, Ann's going to have a real church wedding! Who's going to give the bride away?"

"I am!" said Major Thorne. The plump smiling Flight Surgeon was right in back of her. "We're going to use the groom's college class ring for the ceremony."

Captain Betty Ryan said excitedly, "I'm going to play the wedding march on the organ. And Ann's technician is going to sing *Abide With Me*. And I've sent the news to the Army newspapers, too!"

Cherry learned what else these, and several other, higher-ranking officers were contributing to the cause of romance. Jack and Ann were to have twenty-four hours off, for a honeymoon, come blitz, come battles, come anything. The Brigadier-General commanding this base would move out of his cottage for twenty-four hours and lend it to the honeymooners. The General's aide, a major, not to be outdone, had dispatched a corporal in search of delicacies, wine, and flowers for the honeymoon dinner à *deux*.

Suddenly Cherry remembered Muriel. Their mascot must be present! She hastily telephoned Mrs. Jaynes. Yes, the obliging neighbor would bring the little girl over this afternoon, in her prettiest dress.

There was a last-minute scramble to find the traditional "something old, something new, something borrowed, something blue." Ann's own shoes, a new pair of Cherry's stockings, Gwen's Christmas combs, and a pair of blue garters, solved that.

Cherry was completely out of breath as noon approached, but she remembered one more thing. The masculine contingent had to be made presentable. "'Snails and nails and puppy dogs' tails,'" she muttered laughingly to herself. She knew too well her brother Charlie's life-long reluctance to dress up—and Bunce's tendency *not* to comb his hair. Wade, too, needed an occasional prod. Stopping at the flight technicians' barracks, Cherry sent a soldier in to get Bunce.

"H'lo, Miss Cherry!" the lanky boy grinned at her happily. "Isn't it swell about Miss Ann? I'm goin' to be there with bells on! All us technicians, especially her own corpsman. We'll all be there!"

"Bunce Smith," Cherry said sternly, "comb your hair, scrub your face, shine your shoes, and throw away that chewing gum."

"Pooh, you don't scare me! But all right, I sure will look pretty."

Cherry crossed the field and threw pebbles at Wade's window in the pilots' barracks. When Wade stuck his head out, she repeated similiar instructions.

Wade looked aggrieved. "You know what I'm doing this very minute? I'm pressing my best uniform, you bully! Anything I can do to help?"

"No thank you. G'bye."

He said, "Wait—I have news," and slammed the window shut. He came racing out, took her arm, and walked her along the path under the old trees.

"Cherry, my transfer came through! And the bomber I'm getting—a brand-new B-17, a honey—she's on the field and getting *your picture* painted on her. Right now!"

Cherry gulped. She really was touched. "That's a wonderful compliment, Wade. I'm honestly glad that you're getting your heart's desire."

"No more fuming now," Wade grinned. "No more inaction."

Cherry gasped. "So you call what we've been doing 'inaction'? Wade Cooper, I don't think I'll ever get used to you!"

Wade's brown face crinkled. He blurted out, "I was sort of hoping you'd get used to me. You know, Cherry, I'm pretty fond of you. And I've heard tell that nurses make the best wives and mothers."

Cherry trembled a little, but strolled on at his side calmly enough. "Oh, Ann's wedding is just making you feel romantic."

"No, I'm serious. Doesn't sound like it because I have to say it fast. Fast—we're in the Army and we haven't much time."

"Wade, dear, that's just it: we're in the Army. In the Army, you think you fall in love, when you're only homesick, I guess. Let's not fall in love. Not in the Army. Because soon you'll be transferred, and I may be transferred if—uh—well, or we'll move, or—and if we were in love, it would be tougher."

Wade strode along slowly with his head bent. "Sure, love in a combat zone is a bad gamble. All right, we'll skip it. Guess I was a little hasty."

'Why, Captain, you know your heart doesn't belong to me, but to that B-17!"

Cherry looked affectionately at this tall, sinewy young man, tanned by the wind and sun of high skies. It had been a happy time, working with Wade Cooper. He was, beneath his cool breath-taking nerve, beneath his ready humor, a touchingly sweet, gentle and simple person.

Cherry said, "Wade, now that we're going off in different directions, I want to ask you a very, very, very serious question! Did you honestly fly in China and Russia and Africa and all those places you said? Or were those just tall tales to make the boys feel better? Tell the truth."

"Sure I did!" Wade said. "Why did you find that so hard to believe? What's so remarkable about a record like that? Now you tell me something—about Mark Grainger."

Cherry cleared that up for him—omitting to mention that her own Army standing still hung in the balance.

"So everything is settled? That's fine." Wade started to whistle *One Meat Ball*. Cherry knew he was happy.

They went on to lunch. The meal was a snatch-grab. No one cared: all the nurses and pilots were too excited about Ann's wedding. It was only two hours off now. In the midst of the happy confusion, Gwen wormed her way over to Cherry with a big package and a message.

"Gosh, Cherry, the Flight Surgeon sent word that the Brigadier-General himself wants to see you right after the wedding ceremony!"

She shoved the package into Cherry's arms. Cherry stood there petrified. Here came her troubles—and at such a moment!

"Aren't you going to open it?" The girls crowded around.

"Oh. Of course."

It was from Charlie—a perfectly beautiful flowered silk dress that he had picked up heavens knew where. There was a note enclosed. "Happy Birthday," he wrote, "a little late." Cherry cheered up immensely. Blessings on her brother!

Just then, Muriel arrived with Mrs. Jaynes. The child looked so happy and untroubled, and so doll-like in a little pink dress, that Cherry's heart contracted.

"Am I going to be married?" Muriel inquired.

"Not today, dear," Cherry explained. "You're going to help Ann get married."

"I'd rather help you."

"Well, you can help me get ready in my very best uniform!"

Ann's wedding went off with great beauty and dignity. Ushers seated the nurses in the garlanded pews on one side of the chapel, the pilots on the other side, the corpsmen behind their nurses. Everyone wore full military regalia. The organ pealed forth and filled the chapel with music. Jack stood waiting with the chaplain at the flower-decked altar.

Then Ann came slowly down the aisle, on the Major's arm. Everyone turned. Tears started to Cherry's eyes. She had never seen Ann look so beautiful nor so moved, as she did in her trailing, white gown, walking slowly toward Jack. They had waited for each other for nearly three years, Cherry remembered.

The music faded, ceased.

Cherry heard the low voice of the chaplain, reciting the wedding service. Then his questions, and she heard the even lower responses of the bridal couple as they stood before the altar.

"I, Ann Evans, take thee, John Powell ..."

"... to love, honor, and cherish..."

"... till death do us part."

"... till death do us part," Ann echoed.

And then the chaplain's pronouncement, and Ann in Jack's arms, and it was over! Everybody laughed and talked, and poured out of the pews to wish them happiness.

They all followed the happy bride and groom out of the chapel, and trooped over to mess hall for the reception. Cherry was in back of Ann, holding up her train, when she sharply recalled that she had an appointment to see the Brigadier-General! Now! She felt almost sick. She went on happily to the hall, though, with the rest, planning to slip away unnoticed. Only Gwen knew something was up.

There was no need to slip away. The Brigadier-General himself had come to congratulate Lieutenant and the very new Mrs. Powell. It was a real honor to have this busy and important man present. When he told Ann and Jack how happy he was about this, the first marriage at his base, he sounded as if he genuinely meant it.

In fact, this soldierly elderly man was enjoying himself among the young wedding guests. Since he showed no signs of leaving, Cherry wondered when she was to report to his office. Finally, she reluctantly went over to ask Major Thorne and Captain Betty Ryan, who were standing together. She had to face it sooner or later.

Major Thorne's eyes twinkled. "The General will see you. Just stay awhile at the party yourself. But first, Captain Ryan has an order for you."

Captain Betty Ryan, to Cherry's consternation, looked troubled. The trim small Chief Nurse had to clear her throat uncomfortably before she could bring herself to speak. Finally she said:

"Lieutenant Ames, I'm awfully sorry to have to tell you this. You've been a good flight nurse—an excellent one, in fact. I'm sorry to have to lose you."

"I expected this, ma'am," Cherry said. Her heart was like lead. A fine ending!

"Well, that makes it a bit easier to tell you." The Chief Nurse looked relieved. "After all, you can at least be proud of your work record. You've flown almost every day, except for rest periods. You've flown five combat missions, and that's a lot."

Cherry said miserably, "Captain Ryan, don't try to soften it. I know I'm in disgrace for breaking regulations."

"Disgrace? What are you talking about?" smiled Captain Ryan.

"Breaking what regulations?" Major Thorne demanded.

Cherry told them how she had picked up an unidentified civilian in a combat area and flown him back to England.

"Oh." Major Thorne said dryly. "You'll be hearing more about that particular flight from the General."

"That's just what I'm afraid of, sir," Cherry said.

"May I finish what I was saying?" Captain Betty Ryan continued briskly, "As I said, you have made quite enough flights for awhile, even for a nurse in good physical condition. But that hospital report on you—" She shook her head. "Did you realize you have a badly strained back and also show signs of dangerous fatigue? I am sorry, my dear, but I must herewith order you home."

"Oh no!" Cherry wailed. "Please, Captain!"

Major Thorne said gently, "Your orders are to go home and catch up on your sleep, my girl."

Cherry was heartbroken.

"Maybe this will console you," Captain Ryan said. "You're to fly your mission home in a C-54, attending the wounded. Aren't you excited? From Prestwick to Newfoundland to New York. You'll be in New York day after tomorrow!"

Cherry gave a faint shriek. "Please, ma'am, when—when do I start for Prestwick?"

"Tomorrow at dawn."

"But it's five o'clock in the afternoon now! Oh, Major, Captain, I want to go on being a flight nurse," Cherry pleaded. "I've trained—I have experience—"

"But you're worn out," Major Thorne reminded her. "Don't feel badly, Lieutenant. There are few young women who can stand up under the gruelling strain of combat flight nursing for very long periods at a time. You've done well. You were just unlucky to have strained your back."

Cherry mumbled, "Yes, sir, but—but can't I go on being an Army nurse?"

"Certainly you can. But no more combat nursing for you. That means you can transfer into Army nursing within the United States. In the camps—or in the reconditioning hospitals for our wounded—"

"I'd like to go on helping our wounded soldiers, sir."

"Well, you can! You're badly needed at home."

Captain Ryan teased, "Aren't you really, deep down, just a little glad that you'll be home again?"

Cherry supposed she was, after she sat down alone in a corner and thought over things. The wedding party went on gaily all around her, while she tried to digest the news. Home! It meant she would see Hilton and her family again, very soon. She would wear the dress Charlie had just sent her—she might even see her adored brother. He would be the flier of the family now. Well, maybe one flier in a family was enough. Her mother would be relieved. And Midge—she mustn't forget Midge, who was—incredibly—sixteen and a half now and almost a Cadet nurse. And Dr. Joe! Now she could tell Dr. Joe in person what Mrs. Eldredge's mysterious worry was, and that it was all ironed out. Home in an American Army hospital, perhaps to treat the very same soldiers whom she had rescued and first sent on their way to America.

"Why are you sitting in a corner all by yourself?"

"And looking so glum?"

Gwen and Wade stood before her.

Cherry sighed and looked up. "I have my orders home."

"What! I don't believe it!"

"But you haven't christened *The Cherry* yet!"

"Flight Three!" Gwen summoned their own little group. Aggie and Elsie and Maggie hurried over, the bride too. "Cherry is going home!" Gwen announced.

They were speechless, then all chattered at once. Cherry smiled at them regretfully—they six had enjoyed a unique friendship. The Army was too full of goodbyes. Bunce was at her side now, too choked up to talk. Wade was not talking either, just tightly clasping her hand.

"You'd think I was dead," Cherry giggled. "I'm only going home. I'll see you kids again."

Suddenly the Brigadier-General's aide called out, "Atten-*tion*!"

The whole room fell sharply silent and everyone snapped to stiff attention.

"Will Lieutenant Cherry Ames please step forward?"

Cherry went up to the General in a daze and saluted. She stood there waiting.

The General took from his aide a typewritten paper. He looked at Cherry and to her utter surprise, read this citation:

"For distinguishing herself by meritorious achievement while participating in an aerial flight, to Lieutenant Cherry Ames, the United States Air Medal. Her professional skill, courage, and high sense of service reflects great credit upon herself and the Armed Forces of the United States."

The Brigadier-General then pinned the medal on Cherry's jacket. He smiled at her proudly as he did so. Cherry smiled back with enormous happiness and relief. A citation! The Air Medal! She was going home in triumph.

She was so happy and stunned she barely heard the applause of her friends and comrades, and the surge of their congratulations. Ann and Gwen kissed her. She held them both close for an instant. Then Bunce was pumping her hand—and Muriel was begging to wear a medal, too, and offering Cherry her cherished Lilac to take home—when Wade whisked the whole party out to the field to see his new bomber, just ferried in.

The ground crew rolled the mighty bomber out of the hangar. Painted on her fuselage was a bright-colored likeness of Cherry. Her name was painted, too, in big, bold, bright red letters! Beaming, Cherry broke a bottle of pop on a machine gun in its nose, and pronounced:

"I christen you *The Cherry*—and see that you bring the flyers safely home!"

In the general gaiety, Cherry slipped off from Ann and Jack and Gwen, from little Muriel who held Wade's hand on one side and Bunce's on the other. She walked by herself into the gathering dusk. The roar of bombers swelled over her head. Now she was leaving the sound of fighting planes; saying good-bye to these serene trees and this ancient, stalwart British island; putting an end to the teas before Mrs. Eldredge's fire. No more, this gypsy existence of flight and danger and mystery. For the last time, she had flown over England, lying on her stomach by the window, watching their plane's moon shadow, tagging along over the hills below.

How happy she had been here, being partners with Wade, and with Bunce to help her! How deeply satisfying to bring suffering men back to safety and care! What exciting times she had had on this thoroughly remarkable little island!

Cherry turned to the west, where the sun was sinking and home lay. Before a rosy brick ivy-covered building, the American flag was fluttering down at day's end. Cherry watched her flag, and thought:

"Home! I'm going home! I'm not really leaving the Army. I'll just be starting afresh—at home!"